A Groom for Nora

Book #4
Sons of Nora White

CYNDI RAYE

Table of Contents

.... 1

A Groom For Nora 2

Copyright 4

Dedication 7

Chapter 1 10

Chapter 2 21

Chapter 3 34

Chapter 4 44

Chapter 5 52

Chapter 6 63

Chapter 7 71

Chapter 8 80

Chapter 9 88

Chapter 10 95

A Groom For Nora

by

Cyndi Raye

Sons Of Nora White

Book #4

---

1. http://www.CyndiRaye.com

Cover art by Silver Heart Studio

Dedication

This book is dedicated to my wonderful readers for asking for this story!

A special thanks to Sandy and Trudy for all your help!

Chapter 1

Nora stopped the wagon at the Wichita Falls livery. She nodded to the young man who came out to greet her.

"Welcome, ma'am, can I take your rig?"

"Yes, I'll be staying overnight. Thank you, sir."

"Name's John. Most call me Big John."

Once she was on the ground, she understood why they called him by that name. He was quite tall. She smiled at him while shaking out her skirts. He was a handsome young man and wondered if Miss Addie sunk her matchmaker claws into him yet. The thought made her smile. She was anxious to have tea with the extraordinary woman.

"Thank you, Big John. My name is Nora White. Now, have you seen my ranch hand? His name is Matt and he loves food. I'm sure the first thing he asked you is where to get something to eat. I sent him ahead about an hour ago to make sure I was able to get a room for tonight."

"Yes, ma'am, er, Miss White. He said to tell you he reserved two rooms at Miss Addie's boarding house and he'll be down town at Jenna's Café when you come in."

"I suppose he is still there. Matt loves to eat. Why, I can barely keep my supply filled but he's been that way since he was hired by Rusty quite a few years back."

Big John tipped his hat. "I'll be stabling your horse for you. Anything else?"

"No thank you." She paid the livery fee, picked up one of her light carpet bags and made her way toward the boarding house. Thoughts of Rusty standing there, looking so forlorn as she was leaving crossed her mind.

He had always been such a steadfast part of her life. When her husband died, Rusty had been there as she fell apart. He had helped her get back on her feet without showing signs of weakness in front of her children or the rest of the hands.

Even though this journey she was now on was not permanent, she'd miss seeing him each day. He was a good friend.

Miss Addie waved from the front porch. "Miss White. I'm so glad to see you!"

Nora made her way across the street and onto the porch. "I'm so looking forward to a cup of your fine tea."

The older woman looked pleased. "Well, no worries, let's get you settled while the water heats up."

Nora was shown a room at the top of the stairs by one of the young girls in Miss Addie's care. "My name is Matilda. If you need anything, please let me know. You'll have a good hearty breakfast and supper with your room."

"I'll be looking forward to supper this evening, thank you." She washed up then made her way down the stairs that led into the parlor, a lovely room with various sitting arrangements and a nice size window where patrons were able to see outside.

She caught her image in the oval shaped mirror hanging on the wall. Nora never worried about her hair or the way she looked. She was a rancher who got dirty and didn't entertain often. She stopped for a moment, pushed the loose strands away from her face, tucking the dark hair behind her ears.

"You look fine as you are," a voice, plain as day came out of nowhere.

Nora turned to the person sitting in a chair by the stairs. "I'm sorry? Are you addressing me?"

The man had been reading the newspaper. He placed it on his lap and smiled, a slow deliberate one that showed nice, clean, even teeth. His moustache was nicely waxed over his top lip and curled up at each side.

Nora had seen his kind before. Charmers. They thought all they had to do was smile at a lady and she'd swoon. Nora White didn't swoon but she wasn't going to refuse a compliment no matter who it came from.

The man stood, the paper fell to the floor, forgotten. He took her hand and bowed. "My lady, you have brightened this room with your presence. My name is Jonathan Blakely. Welcome to Miss Addie's boarding house."

Nora felt as if she needed to curtsy but smiled instead, pushing the silly thought away. "Why, thank you Mr. Blakely. I'm Nora White. Now if you will excuse me, I'll be having tea with Miss Addie."

"Will I see you again?" he asked, raising a hand in the air.

Nora shrugged. "I'm staying here a day or so, Mr. Blakely. Perhaps we will see you at supper."

"Wonderful. I'll see you then."

Nora shook her head. The man was handsome in his own right and made her laugh. She hadn't done that in ages. Actually, she didn't remember a man putting a smile on her face since her husband Robert was alive. Except for Rusty. He was always making her laugh but they were old friends.

"There you are, dear. Have a seat." Two tea cups were setting on the place mats on the large table. Miss Addie sat down across from her asking about her day. She made small talk for some time.

"Nora, if I may call you that? What are you doing here? Don't you have a ranch to run?"

Miss Addie was observant if not blunt and to the point. She had found mail order brides for two of Nora's sons. It had been quite the adventure watching them get married. "I wanted to stop by to inform you that your chosen picks were matches. As you know Luke, my first born, and Abigail are about to have a baby. Adam is happily married to Melody, his life long best friend and Samuel, well, I'm sure you heard about that fiasco."

Miss Addie nodded. "Of course I did. There's nothing secret here in Wichita Falls or the surrounding area. His bride is quite the adventurer. It probably had a lot to do with her father and uncle being gold miners themselves in their day."

"You may be right. All I know is they are all happily married. I wanted to stop here and thank you for choosing such wonderful wives for my boys. I can leave now for my own adventure without worry."

Miss Addie placed her tea cup on the table, making sure not to spill the liquid on the lace tablecloth. "Oh, an adventure? Tell me, dear. What are you planning?"

She smiled. "I know we don't know each other well but you are a fine upstanding citizen here in Wichita Falls. Saying that, I know I can put my own future in your hands."

"That's odd. I thought you had a future. Watching your boys get married and running your ranch. When we last spoke that was your deepest desire."

"Things have changed, Miss Addie. My three boys kept a secret from me for over ten years. Let's put it this way, my departed husband was not who I thought he was."

"Oh, dear. I'm sorry. If you would like to talk about him, I have a good ear for listening."

She shrugged. "I suppose there isn't much to say in his regard. He did me wrong. I doubt I'll ever be able to forget what he did, but forgive him, I'm not even sure I can do that. He's dead ten years now. I've been a widow long enough."

"Are you thinking of remarrying?"

"I'm not sure. I told my sons and their wives I was going on my own journey to think things through. The truth is I don't want to be away from the ranch. It is my home, I love waking up to the glorious sunrise and all God has given me, working all day and then seeing my boys and the ranch hands and feeding them a good meal. After supper, we all sit on the porch and talk or sing and it fulfils my life, keeps me whole."

"Then why change anything?"

"I am tired of being alone. I never gave another man a thought until I heard the news of the secret my husband kept and his treachery. I was so mad I hid in my room for five days." Nora laughed. "Every single person on that ranch came knocking on my door, trying to get me to come out. But the truth is, I didn't want to face anyone. I wanted to think. Which was impossible with everyone at my door day and night."

"So this journey you are on now is going to help you decide whether to remarry?"

Nora nodded, sipping her tea. "I suppose so. All these years I stayed faithful to my husband, mourning his loss, making sure I did right by his boys. There was never a question of my loyalty to his honor. Finding out he was not honorable as well is crushing to the human spirit. I knew he was unfaithful and he asked for forgiveness. What I didn't know was he fathered twins to the widow next door and never confessed that part."

"I'm so sorry, Nora."

"As I am. I announced to everyone at the ranch I was going on my own adventure, that I needed time for myself. There were plenty of sad and tear-filled faces as I left but I felt as if I had no choice. I need to figure out my next move, the final leg of this journey on earth so to speak."

"It appears someone is making sure you are taken care of."

Nora frowned. "Whatever do you mean?"

"The young man who came in here earlier to secure your rooms. Is he your escort?"

"Yes, he is a trusted ranch hand. Rusty insisted I don't go it alone. He was right. I passed quite a few wretched, shoddy looking scoundrels along the trail here."

"Who is Rusty?"

"Rusty is my oldest, dearest friend, the man who wouldn't let me fall apart when my husband Robert died. He stood by my side through the years. He is my right hand man on the ranch."

Miss Addie clasped her fingers together, nodding in a knowing way.

"What? Why are you giving me that look?"

"I observe things, Nora. I'm very good at it if I must toot my own horn. You say you are thinking of finding a suitor possibly for a marriage in the future? Well, I say sometimes things are right in front of you without even realizing."

Was Miss Addie addle-minded? She had been doing matchmaking for a long, long time. Nora had heard all the stories herself even though she didn't live in town. Was she insinuating Rusty was a possible suitor?

She had been by Rusty's side for so long and depended on him all of these years as strictly a friend that a romantic interest never entered her mind. Or did it and she was denying her feelings because of her loyalty to a dead husband who was not faithful? Her eyes opened wide as she recalled how he'd bring her a single flower from the garden. Or, pull out her chair at the supper table. There were so many little hints that she never gave it much thought. She had been caught up in her own sad world.

"I believe it's true, dear Nora."

"It can't be. Our friendship is a long, mutual one, more like a brother and sister."

"Are you sure?"

Nora didn't know how to answer. The realization that Rusty and her? Oh, my! Had he been in love with her all these years, lying in wait until she came to her senses? "It can't be! Impossible?"

"I don't mean to intrude on your conversation," the man with the wax moustache announced as he interrupted their talk, "Perhaps I may be a possible suitor?"

Nora pushed her chair back. "Thank you for the tea, Miss Addie. I believe I'll go find Matt. Nice day to you, Mr. Blakely."

Mr. Blakely opened his mouth then closed it like a fish out of water. She didn't even acknowledge his awful remark as she brushed by to go out the front door.

Her legs were moving as fast as they were able as she shot down the porch steps and made her way to the café. She was certain Matt would still be there eating. Where there was food, Matt was close by.

How dare Miss Addie accuse Rusty of being in love with her! Rusty! He was her dearest friend. They had spent over a lifetime of hard times and good times, watching the children grow up into fine young men. She gasped. He had always been there for her and the boys, just like a husband should have been.

She walked faster as the thought of Robert's deceit rang through her head. He had been her heart and soul for so long until he up and died. Nora never thought he would betray her trust. It had come as quite the shock.

And yet it hadn't hurt as much as everyone thought it would. Her boys kept the fact he had twin sons, thinking she would be devastated to know. Had she always known somewhere deep down?

"Miss Nora, there you are!"

Matt hurried towards her. "You won't believe the food they have in the café. Want to go in for something to eat?"

Nora shook herself, realizing there was no use thinking about the past. What was done was done. She was a different person today. She'd survive. Alone if need be. "Matt! Are you still hungry?"

"Not so much but there is a beautiful woman in that café. Imagine this, food and a lovely girl!"

She patted his hand. "We better get you back to the boarding house. Come along, Matt."

He tucked her hand into his elbow, taking his time as they made their way back. It was a nice walk. Matt was attentive, doing his job as Rusty had instructed.

Rusty had begged her to take someone along. He had said they didn't deserve to be worried about her well-being while running the ranch in her absence. She remembered how his eyes had looked so tortured at the thought of her leaving. When she had pointed to Matt and said he may go as an escort, she remembered how Rusty cast his eyes down, nodding. He had sighed and gave Matt orders to pack up and get ready to roll out with her. Had Rusty wanted to be in his place? She had been upset about the whole ordeal but remembered how slighted she felt when he didn't insist on coming along himself.

Dear Lord in heaven, was he in love with her?

Was she in love with him?

Were all these years of friendship just a disguise for their love for each other?

"Nora! We're here."

She shook herself again. These moments where clarity was not her friend were starting to become more and more of an issue. "You go on in. I'm going to sit outside on the porch for awhile."

"Okay, I'll see you in a bit. I wonder if I might get a glass of lemonade or maybe a piece of the cake I saw cooling earlier." She shook her head at Matt. He was always looking for the next sweet food.

Nora had never known herself to be confused. She always made firm decisions which always benefited the ranch and everyone involved. Nora knew what she was doing when it came to her boys, her ranch and her family.

When it came to her love life, it was obvious she hadn't fared well. What had gone wrong in her first marriage that he had looked at someone else? She stared at the hands in her lap. They were hard working, the nails short, some chipped and the skin wrinkled at times, but she was proud of the way she worked hard to keep things going. Had running a ranch for all its worth cost her the one thing every woman longed for, a faithful husband?

Had Robert looked upon her as plain? Had she worked so hard to keep up with him on the ranch she neglected herself? Was that why he turned to Widow Young? In her desire to see the ranch succeed, had she been blind to his actions?

Another person sat beside her on the porch swing. Without missing a beat, she accepted a glass of lemonade from Miss Addie. "Your escort is enjoying a slice of cake and some lemonade. I thought he was at the café?"

Nora laughed. "He was there admiring Jenna it seems."

"Yes, everyone loves that woman. It's a wonder she is still single."

"Perhaps you can use your capabilities and find her a groom."

Miss Addie nodded, a thoughtful look on her face. "If there was more of a need in Wichita Falls for grooms, I'd already have that set in motion. Unfortunately, there are more women than men right now. However, I'm not affronted if asked to find a person of the female gender a possible groom. It has its possibilities, doesn't it?"

"It may be likely. Perhaps in the future."

Miss Addie took a sip of her drink. "Where are you headed next?"

Nora shrugged. "I'm not sure. I don't want to get too far from the ranch even though I told everyone I'm going on a grand adventure. I needed space to think and to clear my mind."

"Fortunately for you, Nora, you've done well on your ranch and can afford to take time away. Now, why not have a grand adventure? Go to Dallas, visit the newest restaurants, take in a show, enjoy yourself in the city. You do have an escort that loves to eat. He'd keep himself busy with all the fine dining."

Nora grinned. "It may be just what I need!"

<> <>

The buggy was loaded and ready to go. Miss Addie stood on the porch. Nora gave her a big hug. "Thank you, I'm going to follow your advice and take a grand adventure after all. First, I'm going to stop and visit Pastor Murphy in Coopers Ridge and make sure there isn't a spark of, let's say, any romantic flairs there. Then, I'm off to the big city."

"You will be fine, Nora. I'm glad you are doing this. It is well deserved."

"Thank you." Nora wasn't sure if she deserved this trip but she was going to take this time as a sabbatical of sorts. She was no nonsense, could live off the land or in a hotel, it didn't much matter. They would find shelter along the way and camp out under the stars if it was a clear night. This would be fun. Matt may not think so but she planned to enjoy every single moment.

Would she miss Rusty?

She already did.

Only two days gone and she felt this tugging at her heart to go back home.

No.

She wanted this time to herself.

"Giddy-up."

The wagon left Wichita Falls with Miss Addie waving from the front porch. Jenna happened to exit her small café as their wagon passed by, a bundle in her arms. She raised her voice to get Matt's attention, who stopped the moment she called.

"Well, I'll be!" Nora realized there was a bit of romance going on between her ranch hand and the owner of the café. He stayed behind to speak with Miss Jenna.

Matt caught up ten minutes out.

"I'm sorry, Miss Nora. Look what we got for our trip. There's fresh bread and churned butter, two pastries, and even some fried chicken. That Jenna sure is a good cook."

"It is kind of her to supply us with such wonderful food."

He shrugged. "I think she likes me."

Nora laughed out loud. "I think you like her, too."

"Maybe."

Nora watched as he pulled a large chunk of bread and began to eat, chewing noisily. "Where we headed?" he asked, his mouth so full she barely understood his words.

"To Coopers Ridge."

"Might be some ruffians there. I'm not sure it's a good idea."

"It will be fine. Don't you worry, the pastor of the church will keep us safe. We are good friends."

Matt frowned. "That's all well and good but Coopers Ridge is no place for a lady."

Nora studied Matt. "Why is that? I've been going to church in Coopers Ridge for the last year and a half and no one has stopped me in all this time. What are you not telling me, young man?"

Matt looked uncomfortable.

"Matt, spill the beans!"

"Yes, ma'am. Rusty said and I'll repeat his exact words. Do not allow Miss Nora in Coopers Ridge, that dog-gone pastor has the fancy for her."

Nora clasped her hands tighter on the reins. "Oh, he said that, did he?"

Matt nodded before stuffing the rest of the bread in his mouth. Probably so he wasn't able to answer any more questions. Nora watched as his cheeks pinked. He realized too late he told her that Rusty was a wee bit jealous of the pastor.

All these things going on behind her back and she had no idea!

It was time Nora White took a hold of her life. She was going to Coopers Ridge, come hell or high water and Rusty didn't have to like it one iota! She was her own woman. Always had been. No man would tell her what she could cynd and could not do, or where she should or shouldn't go. No sir, not Nora! Not any more! Not ever!

Chapter 2

The path to Coopers Ridge was filled with mud, slinging it hard against the wagon wheels. It looked as if it had rained for more days than none, causing the road to be muddier than usual. Nora was careful as she drove the horses and not let it rattle her.

The small town was not that far from the White Ranch and she had always rode this way every single Sunday for the past year and a half. When Nora took off the other day, she rode towards Wichita Falls first and now was backtracking to Coopers Ridge. It didn't make sense but she didn't want to make any sense.

"We may have wanted to come this way first before it rained yesterday," Matt mentioned for the fourth time today.

She twisted her body towards his voice. He was behind her and by the looks of his puffy cheeks, he was making sure there would be no bread left when they stopped.

It didn't matter, Matt was good to her. He had faithfully rode alongside of her without complaining up until now. Even if Rusty had been the one to give the order to do so.

That Rusty was going to get a piece of her mind when she got home! He had always been so caring, telling her if she needed to take a trip he would make sure the ranch was taken care of so she need not worry. This whole time he had given Matt orders on where she was to go and who she was allowed to see!

If that didn't rattle her then she didn't know what would. He had a few thinks coming his way!

In spite of being mad at Rusty, a decisive smile crossed her cheeks. When they got to Coopers Ridge she was going to have a few of her own surprises. That would show Rusty he wasn't going to run her life!

The church steeple came into view. Coopers Ridge was one long street. The town butted up against one side of the ridge while an open prairie was seen for miles on end on the other side. Nora was glad to be there, she was tired of riding.

Plus, it would be nice to see Pastor Murphy. He had always been kind to her, even if he was a bit rough around the edges. Every Sunday she looked forward to hearing his sermon. He wasn't bad to look upon either. Tall and dark with a gun belt slung low on slim hips. For a middle-aged man he was quite handsome. The ladies all flocked to church from all over the neighboring ranches in order to try to convince him to be their suitor. It had been fun watching these ladies but now she wondered if perhaps she had been wanting the same thing.

He looked more like an outlaw until he stood in the pulpit, talking about the Lord as if he knew him personally. Some of his sermons gave her goosebumps. It was the reason she had everyone wear their Sunday best each week and ride across the ridge to attend church. Now that she thought about things, she did recall Rusty grumble each week they headed out this way.

But he was faithful. Each week no matter how much he complained, Rusty sat beside her on the wooden bench even if she had to nudge him now and again when he snored.

"Mrs. White, what a pleasure!"

The pastor was walking down the street towards his saloon, a bible in his hand when he noticed her arrival.

She waved, slowing her rig at the sight of him. "Hello, Pastor Murphy."

"What brings you to Coopers Ridge on a week day?"

"I'm visiting before heading to the big city."

"Oh, is there something I need to pray about for you, Mrs. White?"

"Well, we can discuss that later. For right now, I'd like to settle somewhere. Is there a hotel or boarding house available?"

Pastor Murphy glanced at Matt, nodding to the young man. He was still chewing on something, Nora didn't know what it was this time.

"Well, there's a few empty rooms above the saloon but I think you'd be better off if you inquire with Mrs. Jorden at the boarding house. I'm sure she can accommodate you both."

"Oh, Matt won't need a room. I'm sending him back to the ranch."

Matt stopped chewing. She finally got his undivided attention. "What?"

She turned and nodded. "I appreciate your faithfulness, Matt. I do need you to go back to the ranch and let everyone know I'm fine and where we are off to on the next leg of our journey. I don't want my boys to worry about me. They have enough with their new lives and the ranch."

"But, Rusty said not to let you out of my eyesight."

"Who pays your salary, Matt?" She hated to use that line but it was the truth.

"You do, Miss Nora."

"Well, then. Please go back and let everyone know I'm fine and in good hands." She turned and smiled at the pastor, who looked somewhat confused.

Matt nodded. "Yes, ma'am."

"I'll see you here tomorrow."

Matt turned to go, looking quite upset.

"Matt?"

He turned.

"It's all fine. I promise. Pastor Murphy will let no harm come to me, isn't that right, Pastor?"

He nodded. "Of course, you are in good hands." He looked up and Nora wasn't sure if the pastor was rolling his eyes or meant she was in God's hands.

<> <>

"What do you mean you left her in Coopers Ridge! That place is a haven for outlaws and desperadoes!"

Luke intervened. "I wouldn't say it's that bad, Rusty. Pastor Murphy has cleaned up Coopers Ridge. He only allows folks who have been reformed to live there. Otherwise, they are sent away."

"Humph! He was an outlaw himself once!"

Adam shook his head. "Rusty, the pastor named the town after himself. His first name is Cooper. He changed that old place and built a nice town."

Rusty shook his head. He didn't understand what Nora saw in the pastor even if he did clean up the town, making it a place where goods were traded and people were able to start over again. It just galled him something fierce that Nora was always wanting to go listen to his sermons. He caught her looking at the pastor with googly eyes plenty of times. That's when he'd snore so loud she took her eyes off the pastor and paid attention to him.

"Every single week for the last year and a half I trudged along, riding on that buggy with her to Coopers Ridge to listen to that dang blasted man and now he's going to try to steal her away!"

"Rusty!" Luke was trying not to laugh. Rusty saw how he turned his face away, a grin on his face. Well, it wasn't funny.

"What?" Adam was doing the same thing.

Samuel piped up. "Rusty, you need to calm down."

He turned to Nora's boys. With hands on his hips, he barked at them all. They were standing in the barn, watching him have a conniption fit at the thought of Nora wanting another man. "What do you three care? You have your new lives and pretty wives to keep you company. My world is gone! She left, drove right out of the yard and in to the arms of a dog-gone do-gooder!"

Matt's eye widened. "Hey, Rusty, I didn't come here to get you all stirred up. I have to go back tomorrow. She's not planning on staying there long. We're headed to Dallas to see some shows. She plans on having a grand adventure, I heard her tell Miss Addie."

Rusty turned and stared down Matt. "Dallas! Over my dead body. Boy, you are back to work right here on the ranch! I'll be the one to escort Nora to Dallas!"

Matt grinned. "Well, okay. But, I'll have you know she told me your not my boss, she is. So I hate to inform you that you can't be bossing me around."

"Well, she ain't here and I can kick your behind right into that bunk house, kid! Now don't be giving me lip. I'm the one who will escort her, understand?"

Matt took off without looking back, heading towards the bunkhouse. He stopped to grab a wrapped bundle from his saddlebag before scooting to his bunk.

Luke and Adam laughed at the way Matt behaved. "For not being his boss, Matt sure did follow Rusty's orders, didn't he?" Adam mumbled.

Samuel made a face. "So, what is Ma doing? Do you think it was safe to leave her in Coopers Ridge?"

Rusty declared war. "I swear if she is in any danger I'll horsewhip young Matt."

"Settle down, Rusty. You've sure been cranky since Ma left," Samuel told him.

Rusty knew he was on the grumpy side lately. He took a deep breath, determined to slow down his heart rate. He swore it felt like someone was inside punching him. "I'm sorry boys. All of you, forgive me. It's just, well, with Nora gone, things aren't the same."

Luke flung an arm around his shoulder. "Then go bring Ma home, Rusty."

"She wants an adventure." Those simple words she spoke to him the day she left had gotten to him somewhere deep in his gut. She wanted excitement, an adventure. Had he been a disappointment to her? Why, he was pretty happy with their mode of entertainment here on the ranch. What more did she need?

Adam flung an arm over his shoulder. Next, Samuel closed in. "We love you, but you can be pretty lame-brained! So, Rusty, give her an adventure! She wants to go to Dallas, take her and show her the adventure of a lifetime!"

Maybe these boys were right. Rusty grinned. Why not! "What about the ranch, who is going to be in charge?"

"Rusty! Would you go on now! Get your best suit out and pack your bag. It's time you follow some dreams, too! You are the only person we trust with our Ma, no offence to Matt. We have the ranch under control. We can run it in our sleep."

"You better not even try. Promise you'll be out there taking care of things instead of lazing the day away in bed."

"Go on, Rusty. Trust us, we've been doing this a long time. You bring Ma home, we don't want to see her with anyone else except you."

Samuel's word made him feel like he was ten feet tall, not the five foot eleven he stood wearing boots. He gathered a few clean shirts and a pair of britches, careful to fold his Sunday go to meeting suit on the top of the carpet bag. After giving instructions to the rest of the crew, Rusty settled down to get a good nights sleep.

Yep, he was going to give Nora one heck of a surprise. He just hoped he could get to her before that dang pastor used those fancy words on her and cast her under his heavenly spell.

<><>

"Thank you, kindly."

"My pleasure, Miss White. Shall we?" He held out his arm.

Pastor Murphy had collected her from the front porch of the boarding house. He had offered to take her on a delightful tour of the town.

They had walked down the main street, which was the only street in town. They had strolled past store fronts and homes with whitewashed fronts. It wasn't much of an established town but it was a start.

Along the left side of town, the houses almost butted up against a wide ridge. "Why were those houses built so close to the ridge?" she asked him, trying to find something casual to talk about. He wasn't a man of many words. Nora wasn't used to forcing a conversation.

Pastor Murphy looked up where she was staring. "I guess to protect the town if need be. Once you are up there on the ridge you can see anyone coming and going for miles and miles. It seemed like a good place to build."

"I see. So the rumors are true? You are the one who built this town?"

He raised an eyebrow and nodded. "I'm afraid the rumors are true, Miss White. When I saw this land and decided to place my hat here, I didn't want all this for myself. There were a few shabby buildings here, a haven for outlaws to hide out. I was one of them and when I purchased this place, it turned my life around. It was easy to picture a town where those who had once done wrong could right themselves and live in harmony. I dreamed of a sanctuary for those who truly wanted to start over. To live in peace. No one judges here."

She looked around. Several men walked past, nodding to the pastor and tipping a hat to her. "I find your sermons each week are filled with that very thing."

"It keeps the residents on their toes. It doesn't hurt to remind them of the rules, especially those fighting their own souls. I own almost everything here, Miss White. The saloon, the church, all the homes and businesses except for the few I sold. The buildings are leased for one year until the town can be assured the resident will earn an honest living here. Everyone understands and must accept my rules coming in."

"I had no idea. It's a very interesting concept. I understand what it is like to own acres and acres of land. The White Ranch takes over a large area, it's a big responsibility."

"So is Coopers Ridge. It's why I built into the ridge as you can see. This town has to be protected and if there's any trouble, the men can get up on top there and see what is coming at us."

They were standing at the end of Main Street. "It is a smart idea. Tell me, how did Coopers Ridge come about?"

He gazed up at the ridge, the sun beating down on the dusty ground. Nora glanced at his profile, the soft lines under his eyes showing the world a lifetime of living. "When I first saw this land with those two shabby buildings slapped on it, I stood on that ridge for two days, praying, promising God if he would redeem my soul and change my way of thinking, I'd make good on my promise to show mercy on those who need to change their lives. All I had to my name was my horse, a bag full of cash and a sleeping blanket. The next day, I inquired about this piece of property and was able to buy it that very day. From there, it all came together rather easily, registering the plotting out the land and registering the lots so I knew the direction came from up there." He pointed to the clouds.

"God is good to you." She turned to him, placing her other hand on his sleeve. "He saw a great man inside of you with a giving heart and knew you were the right person to fulfil your promises."

Nora almost gasped at the intensity in the pastor's eyes. He turned to look at her, taking a hand and running it across her cheek. His touch was warm but it didn't make her heart race. She did like how soft and loving his touch was and closed her eyes, taking in a deep breath.

His mouth brushed over hers. Her eyes opened wide in surprise at the sudden kiss. Immediately, he took a step back. "I'm sorry, I had to know if there was something there."

She grinned, not slightest bit offended. She hadn't felt a thing when he kissed her. Her only worry was that he had. "And?"

He shook his head. "I'm afraid we are resigned to be good friends."

Nora laughed, tugging at his arm. "Come on, friend, let's go get something to eat at the boarding house. I'll buy you lunch."

"I'll do you one even better! How about I cook you a steak. The saloon is closed until later. I have the best steaks money can buy and there is one with your name on it."

Nora never went inside a saloon before but she had to admit being curious. "Well, as long as it is closed."

"It's a decent place, Miss White. I would not take you there if it weren't. I run an honest place and it's about the only food establishment besides the boarding house for right now."

"Tell me more about your town, Pastor Murphy."

"Only if you call me Cooper."

She smiled. "That's a fine idea, Cooper. Since we have established our friendship, I insist on being called Nora."

"Very well, Nora it is." He held a hand out, guiding her onto the porch of the saloon. "Please join me in a delightful dinner of steak and some fresh bread."

Nora sat in the kitchen area of the saloon, laughing as Cooper made his way around, heating up the stove and grilling two steaks. He even sliced two large pieces of bread and slathered butter over top. She helped him carry the finished plates to one of the tables in the saloon.

It wasn't a bad place. Tables and chairs adorned the room, along with a long wooden bar at the front. Glass cabinets lined the back, filled with bottles and glasses. She wondered how he could be a pastor of a church and a bartender at the same time.

"I bet I can read your mind." Cooper sliced off a piece of steak, placing it in his mouth.

"So you are not only a pastor and own a saloon but a betting man to boot?"

He inclined his head. "I know it seems strange and I think I won this bet. Am I right that you are wondering how I can be both a bartender and a preacher?"

She nodded, taking a small bite of her steak, chewing carefully before answering. "Yes, I believe you won this round. This steak is delicious by the way."

Cooper nodded his thanks. "I sold several buildings here, leased out others and even gave a home or two to some who were destitute and needed a place to hang their hat. So far this town runs smoothly. I keep the saloon under my ownership because I want to provide a decent place for entertainment. I'm afraid if I sell it to the wrong person, debauchery will win out. Does that make sense?"

"It does make sense. God led you here. He allowed the doors to open up and give you the means and the way to start this town. Look at the beautiful church that towers from the entrance of Coopers Ridge. Perhaps instead of a saloon, you turn it into something else."

Cooper raised his glass of water. "I believe you may have given me some good ideas. Thank you, Nora White. You are a Godsend."

"Hardly. I run a ranch. It's never the same, day to day there's always something different happening. Changes are always good, Cooper. Maybe the idea of a saloon in every town is over rated. It's your town, you can do what you want."

"I have alot to think and pray about."

The saloon door swung open. A plump woman, dressed in a long sleeved shirt and long skirt peeked her head in. "Oh, goodness, Pastor it is you!" She slid inside.

Cooper introduced them. "This is Millie, the famous cook of Cooper's Saloon."

"Hello, Millie. A pleasure."

Millie headed towards the kitchen. "Nice to meet you! I best get started. No telling what kind of riff-raff comes through those doors tonight."

Cooper leaned in, laughing softly. "She is one of the worst complainers I've ever met. But she will do anything for anyone. Millie doesn't want anyone to know how big of a heart she has."

Nora raised a brow and scooted her chair back. She wiped her mouth and placed the cloth napkin on the table. "Let me help take these dishes to the kitchen. Should we wash them or will we be in her way?"

"I'll take them back later. The kitchen is her domain. I don't want her to scare you off. It's nice having you around."

"Thank you, Cooper. I've enjoyed your company."

He walked Nora outside where the sun almost blinded her. Holding her hands over her eyes she noticed one of her mares from the ranch in front of the boarding house across the street. "Is Matt back already? I was enjoying myself so much, I hadn't realized it was so late. We are heading to Dallas today, so I must be off. Thank you, Cooper. It was a lovely walk and lunch."

Cooper bowed, took her hand and brought it to his lips. He placed a kiss on the back of her hand in a friendly manner.

She giggled like an old school marm getting her first kiss.

"Hey, what the tar-nation are you doing to her! Get away from her or I'll -"

"Rusty?"

Nora swung towards the voice. Rusty stood on the porch of the boarding house shaking his fist at the two of them. She waved.

"Do I need to defend your honor, Nora?" Cooper stared across the street.

She turned. Placing a hand on his cheek, she smiled. "Thank you again but for some reason Rusty has shown up and he's not too happy. I better go find out what's going on, make sure my sons are fine and the ranch is running smoothly. Matt was supposed to be here instead."

"Let me walk you across the street."

"I am fine, Cooper."

"I insist."

She took Coopers arm as he led her across the street. Rusty came down the steps and stood on the street, madder than she'd ever seen him.

"Rusty? Is everything alright?"

"What are the two of you doing?"

She ignored his question. He almost acted as if he were jealous. "Rusty, it's nice to see you, too."

"Nora." Rusty acknowledged her right before he glared at the pastor. That was unusual for him to be rude, especially to a man of the cloth.

Nora decided it was time to move things along. "Thank you, Cooper. I'll see you in church when I'm back from my adventure."

"Cooper? You are on a first name basis with the preacher?"

Cooper crossed back over the street, his laughter making Nora smile. She believed Rusty was showing signs of jealousy. It was clear now. He thought because he worked at the ranch, well, because he was part of the ranch all these years, he can tell her what to do and who to see. He was behaving like an old mother hen.

Or was it because he had given her money many years ago when the ranch was in trouble? She had tried to pay him back several times over but he called it his investment. Rusty never threw that in her face either. He was a good man. He had been her saving grace. If Rusty hadn't saved her that day, the ranch would belong to someone else.

Her own sons didn't know she bore that secret. Rusty was as much a partner as Nora and the boys. She had the papers made up one time when she was in Wichita Falls. Rusty owned a third of the White Ranch and didn't even know it. Someday she would tell him, but by the looks of things, it would not be now. He was salty at the moment.

Yet, even though she was indebted to him, she was having none of this negativity eluding from him right now. As far as he knew, she was his boss and was able boot him out of a job anytime she aspired to do so. Although they never treated each other like boss and ranch hand, she feared today she may have to put her foot down if he didn't calm down.

"Rusty, if you plan to stand there all day and yell at me you will look awful strange standing in the street all by yourself. I'm done here."

She made her way past him and entered the boarding house. Before she closed the door, she turned. He was staring at her, hands on his hips. Poor Rusty, he looked bewildered, as if he didn't know what to do next. "Go on down to the stable and have our wagon hitched. We'll be leaving within the hour."

Nora closed the door. She steadied herself, pushed back a stray hair behind her ear and sucked in a deep breath. That man was infuriating at times. How dare he question her friendship with the good pastor?

Then a slight smile crossed her face. It was nice having someone care like he did. Because he was here instead of Matt. That meant he cared.

She was going on an adventure.

Who better to have along than the man she had been secretly in love with for all these years.

For now, that would stay her secret.

Chapter 3

Rusty led his horse across the ridge, careful to keep Nora and the wagon in his view. He was burning with anger inside knowing the pastor had spent time with her, in a saloon of all things. What had they been doing in there?

He hadn't said much when he brought her wagon from the livery, instead he helped her with her bags and then on to the bench. From there she took over, holding the reins and leading the wagon away from Cooper's Ridge.

Once they were over the drop, Rusty relaxed. He had second thoughts about taking her to Dallas. What if he wasn't able to entertain her? Heck, he knew how to play a fiddle and stomp to some good banjo music, but put him in the city and he was lost. Why wasn't she happy with the simple life they led?

He was so involved with thinking about Nora, when fat raindrops plopped onto the brim of his hat he began to look around for a place to stop in case the rain brought some bad weather to go with it. A grove of trees would get them out of the rain but only temporary. Then he saw the line shack setting back in a grove of trees. Luckily the leaves had already fallen or they'd have missed it completely.

Nora noticed too. "Over there," she shouted, pointing to the old shack. It didn't look as if anyone had used it in some time but it would keep them dry. There was a lean to for the horses to keep them out of the gusty winds that were stirring in the distance. This may be a quick, windy thunderstorm or last for hours, it was hard to tell.

The wagon rumbled over some wooden planks of a makeshift bridge that led to the small structure. Luckily, there was enough space for their wagon to cross over. A tiny creek below the bridge flowed with spring water, enabling a ranch hand access if he was stuck at the line shack for long periods of time. Rusty got to work while Nora loosened her own mare and led her to the lean-to. She grabbed a wooden box and canvas bag from the back of the wagon then tried to cover herself from the pelting rain. By the time they both got to the shack, the rain was coming down in torrents.

The tiny space had a layer of dust inside. Nora put her things down, then stepped towards the stove, checking to see if there was kindling to start a fire. Rusty helped, finding some small twigs, along with chunks of wood and stuffed them in the belly, stirring the ashes before lighting the stove. They needed a fire to dry their clothes and damp bodies.

"There must be an oil lamp here somewhere." The sky outside had darkened from the storm, causing the inside to be cast in shadows even if it were broad daylight.

Rusty closed the door to the stove and wiped the soot on his pants. "Let's hope this storm blows over soon." He found a lamp on the small rickety table and lit it, causing a glow of light in the darkened room.

"I have provisions in case we're stuck here for awhile," Nora told him, pointing to the box she brought in from the wagon.

"Doesn't look like they use this old shack much. It hasn't been cleaned up in ages."

"I'm about to change that." Nora picked up a broom that sat in the corner. She began to brush away some of the cobwebs. "I'll feel more comfortable if these are gone." She busied herself while Rusty stood out of her way. She was a woman of tall stature, her brown hair pulled back in a stern bun. She always wore comfortable dresses but her beauty shown through. At least Rusty thought so.

He hadn't realized how much he loved her until she left. Even though it hadn't been for that long, Nora had never been away from the ranch for more than a day. He was going to have to tell her how he felt.

Rusty didn't know how to go about these things. He was more comfortable with animals than people. He'd been a ranch hand all his life. Horses and cattle and wide open spaces had been his life.

And Nora.

"What are you staring at?" Nora stopped pushing the broom.

Rusty was caught! He hadn't realized he'd been staring for so long. "Uh, nothing. Didn't get much sleep last night, so, I, ah, yeah, wasn't staring at nothing."

Nora tilted her head, giving him a stern look at first before she turned away to finish her chore.

He let out a sigh of relief. How was he going to tell her that being in such close proximity made his heart race and his blood pump so fast it made him feel like a starving six year old!

Yet, from the looks of things, she wasn't the least bit interested. She kept on pushing that broom as if she didn't have a care in the world.

Rusty sighed. He had to get over this romantic notion stuff. It was making his life miserable. He wanted to have a good relationship with Nora, the one they always had. She was easy to look at but he wanted to hear her laughter, see her smile at the things she loved. He was afraid her going out in the world would make her crave someone else. A tall cowboy that she'd fall in love with. He had to stop her!

He realized she wasn't happy with him right now. Nora always avoided speaking to someone while she contemplated her feelings. He had seen it over and over again over the years. But he had to know why she was upset with him. What had he done to get under her skin? Rusty was going to find out why but now wasn't the time. He'd wait a bit.

After several hours pacing and then checking for the rain to subside with no luck, Nora got up from the wobbly wooden chair to peek out the small hole that was haphazardly cut out as a window. A block of wood was made into a shutter that closed up the hole from the inside with a small hook. Nora unhooked it to peek out. Rainwater pelted through the hole as she slammed the shutter closed. "It doesn't look like we are going anywhere too soon. This thunderstorm is relentless."

Rusty nodded. "We were due for one. Luckily, I have some cards along in my pocket so we don't go stir crazy inside these tiny walls."

"I wasn't expecting to be stuck in a line shack with you, Rusty."

Her soft words melted his heart. Did she mean she was unhappy she was stuck here with him? Or was the slight smile on her face an indication she didn't mind being here with him? He wasn't sure what to make of it so he figured he'd just ask. It was time for a confrontation anyway. "Nora, now you come over here and sit down, it's time we have ourselves a talk."

Nora raised a brow but did as she was told. She placed both hands in her lap, raising her other brow.

Was there a smirk on her face?

Rusty paced back and forth in front of the door. Then he leaned up against the wall, trying to look casual and cool like the other cowboys did when talking to a girl. He crossed his arms over his chest. "You've been short with me, Nora White, and I want to know why."

Nora blushed. "What makes you think I'm upset with you?"

"For one, the way you've been behaving since I showed up in Coopers Ridge. I ain't never seen you act so angry to see me before!"

"Is this why you are anxious? Oh, Rusty, I was happy to see you, except it shocked me that you would want to replace Matt with yourself, considering how much the ranch means to you and how you hate to be away from there."

He shrugged, relaxing his arms. "It ain't the same without you. I figured may as well join you in this adventure of yours."

Nora laughed. "Rusty, you are one sneaky man. I already know that you ordered Matt not to let me out of his sight. When he told me you gave him orders concerning myself, I wanted to horsewhip you I was so mad!" She tried to sound stern but her voice was more angelic than he had ever heard before. It sent shivers down his spine.

"See, I knew you were angry with me! I can read you like a book Nora!"

She stood, placing her hands on her hips and nodded, her voice no longer sweet as sugar. "Yes, I was darn mad at you. I am my own person,

Rusty, I run a big ranch, for Pete's sake. Don't you think I am able to take a trip without you over-lording me?"

"Over what? That's a mighty big word, Nora!"

She shook her head. "Maybe it's time you get off that ranch and get a taste of the outside world. I'm not sure where Matt got to, but you are coming to Dallas with me to get a bit of culture in your old bones." She nodded, seemingly determined to have the final word.

"Of course I am coming along! Why do you think I'm here! I took over Matt's job, which it looks like he didn't do too well. You were cavorting with the pastor in Coopers Ridge in a saloon of all places, and Matt was nowhere around to protect you in case something happened, I, uh, um, darn it, Nora! All he was worried about was the large bundle of food someone gave him. I'll bet he's still feeding from that parcel."

"I'm going to ignore the part about me and the pastor because it is nonsense. He is a kind man who offered to make me dinner. That's all and I'm not sure you have any right to know this information or that I need to explain my actions to you. Speaking of food, I'm going to start making our supper since we don't know how long we'll be here. It looks like we may have to stay the night and head to Dallas at first light."

Rusty was frustrated. She took over the conversation he wanted to have with her and he still wasn't any closer to knowing if he had a chance with her. How did this happen? Then he grinned. Just as it always did with Nora. She ran things on her ranch and obviously with him, too!

She got under his skin from the very first day he met her so many years ago. Her husband Robert had hired him when Rusty was in his prime. Rusty had been quite the ranch hand, taking all the risks on the new ranch the White's had started.

He hadn't been too crazy about Mr. White from the beginning. Robert was shady, always sneaking off to the Young ranch to help the widow, leaving Nora to fend for herself. It had bothered him over the years, but he was a ranch hand and had no say. Her husband swore to her he'd only cheated once, but Rusty knew better and yet he had to keep his trap shut.

Robert was the boss until he got himself killed by those cattle rustlers. In a way it had been a blessing to Nora. She never had to find out how her husband lied and cheated.

Except then the secret came out and that's why they were sitting in a line shack on the outskirts of some other rancher's property waiting for the storm to cease.

Rusty had always suspected the widow got pregnant right after her husband died. He had always thought they were not from her own husband. None of the numbers added up but everyone was grieving so no one had paid much attention. Except for him. When it came to Nora, he had always been careful to make sure no harm came to her. That meant Robert had been cheating with the Widow Young even before she became a widow. What an ugly web of deceit.

Those boys of her had been so young when their Pa died. They all stepped up to the plate, listening when Rusty taught them how to do things they hadn't learned yet. Between Nora, himself and the boys, the White Ranch had grown into a decent sized operation where no one had to ever do without.

Now what were they going to do if Nora goes and finds some big city dandy? There's no way he'd allow that to happen!

If he wanted her then he supposed he'd have to become her suitor and get all fancy and take her to Dallas for a new adventure.

Problem was he had no clue how!

In the meantime, he was going to enjoy every single moment the two spent in this tiny cabin waiting for the rain to cease.

<> <>

Nora gave him a look. "Rusty, you are cheating!"

He dropped the cards on the table and lifted his hands in the air. "How would I do that? You see my hands are empty!" He shook his arms, his eyes lighting up as he teased her.

She was no fool. "Rusty, my old friend, do you know how many times I walked in the barn and stood by watching the lot of you playing poker?"

He nodded, a grin on his face. "Plenty, Nora. I'd say for the last twenty some years you've spent quite a bit of time doing that."

She crossed her arms and leaned back in the chair, stopping when one leg began to wobble. "So, I'd say it is safe to say the card you plan on cheating with is tucked right there in you vest pocket."

"Dag-nab-bit, Nora! You see too much." He pulled the card from the inside of his vest pocket and threw it on the pile. "I quit."

She laughed out loud. "Now don't be a sore loser. If this was a real game you'd be called out cheating like you are."

Rusty sighed. He ran his large rugged hand through his thick hair. Since his hat had been off the hair no longer layed flat but sprung up, flopping down over his forehead. Nora wanted to reach over and push it away but didn't dare.

"It looks like we're staying here for the night."

Instead, Rusty leaned forward and took her hand. "That's not so bad, is it?"

She looked around. "We did a good job sprucing the place up. At least there are no cobwebs to run into."

"You can have the cot," he told her, pointing to a small one in the corner of the room. "I'll make myself comfortable on the wagon outside. The rain stopped but it's too dark for us to leave until morning."

"You'll do no such thing, Rusty! This cabin is big enough for the two of us. Bed down on the floor. There's another blanket in the bag I brought in."

Rusty grinned. "Do you think that's proper?"

Nora had to smile. "Rusty, I think we are too old for being proper. At our age no one is going to force us down the isle with a shotgun."

He agreed. "I guess that wouldn't be so bad."

Her heart lurched. "I'm sorry, what did you say?"

"I said I guess that -"

"Yes, I heard what you said."

"Well, why'd you ask me again?" Rusty stood, rummaging through the bag for the blanket which he pulled out and laid on the floor.

"You said it wouldn't be so bad if someone marched us down the aisle. You mean as in married?"

He shrugged. "Why not. We've known each other forever. Every single day you see my mug and feed me breakfast. The ranch runs by itself because of the two of us. Why, we've been by each others side for the last twenty some years, through every single thing that could go wrong and everything that went right. Why not?"

Nora rolled her eyes. "Oh, Rusty, that sounds like a dull and lifeless proposal. Where's the romance?"

She stood, stretching her legs and arms before heading towards the cot. She put her own blanket down like a sheet since she didn't know who or what was on the cot before now.

"Romance? We ain't never had time for that! But, what the heck! You want romance first? Well, here."

Rusty bent down on one knee and gave her a kiss on the cheek before picking up her hand and bringing it to his lips. He kissed each finger softly and looked her in the eye.

"You and I are a team. We belong together. If a marriage is what you want, I'll be the one to walk you down the aisle and put a ring on your finger. Ain't no one else going to do it!"

Nora knew what he meant but it came out so wrong. She loved Rusty because he was down to earth and said what was on his mind. Except, he wasn't going to get away with a quick proposal and expect her to agree. "What do you mean, ain't no one else going to do it? Rusty? Are you saying no one else will have me?"

"Nora, I mean what I mean. I mean I am the only one for you and if anyone gets in my way, they'll get a boot to their, ah, backside."

Nora watched as his cheeks got red. He was still on one knee but his frustration showed through.

"I wonder if you realize that a girl needs to be courted?"

He let her hand go. "You mean like having a suitor come around and act all lovey-dovey and sport you around town in a three-piece suit?"

"Yes, something like you describe. A woman wants to know a man cares so deeply and that she is the only one for him."

"Dagnabit, Nora! Don't you know by now you are the one! You've been the only one for me from the first time I met you all those years ago but you were married."

This time Rusty stood, pushing his hair back and began to pace back and forth in front of her.

"Oh, Rusty. I truly know you care. And yet, I feel like the adventure would not be complete until we go to Dallas and get us some culture behind these boots." She stuck her foot out to include herself. It was high time the two of them had some fun besides the shenanigans on the ranch.

He turned to stare. "You mean you'll marry me?"

The look on his face was more than enough. She wanted to marry him so bad. She also wanted to be sure he wasn't settling for her because they were so familiar with each other. What if he went to the city and realized there was a whole world out there filled with beautiful women?

She stood and took his two hands in hers and looked him in the eye. "I will marry you under one condition. We both go to the big city and see what else life has for us. I want you to try some new things with me and without me. Will you promise to do so?"

He tilted his head. "What are you asking?"

His steady look caught her off guard but she was serious. "You need to have some fun on your own, see what it's like to have fun, not only with me but by yourself or someone you may enjoy. What if I'm not right for you, Rusty? Don't you want to know? You've been on that ranch for way too long. I am the only person you've ever had a relationship with, even if it was a friendly one."

He sighed. "I've courted my share of women in my day, Nora. Before the ranch, before you. I know what I want. Maybe it isn't me who needs to find out. Maybe it's you."

She felt the blow even if it was from his words. "Maybe it is. I haven't denied I want an adventure. It's why I am going to the city."

He nodded. "Well then, let's get to sleep so we can start fresh first thing in the morning." Rusty squeezed her hands before settling on the hard floor.

It took Nora a few hours before she finally began to tire. Thoughts of her grand adventure rolled in her head like a pair of dice that wouldn't stop. She did love Rusty but the big city was calling out to her.

She was worried. What if it turned out she didn't want to marry Rusty after all?

Chapter 4

Dallas was nothing like she remembered. It had been well over ten years since Nora stepped foot here. Back then, there were roughly three thousand residents. According to the lop-sided sign she read as they entered the city limits, the inhabitants of Dallas were well over seven thousand strong.

This was the first time Nora ever got to stay in the city for longer than a day. The one time Robert brought her here, it was to buy livestock. She had wanted to ride along to see how the operation worked. It turned out to be a good thing she did because after he died she knew exactly what to do to keep the ranch operating. With her knowledge and Rusty's hard work, the White Ranch would not be what it is today.

The sheer size of the buildings alone seemed overwhelming at first. Nora always felt in control whenever she went to town but today it was quite intimidating. After they dropped off the wagon and horses at the livery, giving instructions where to take their belongings, Rusty offered his arm while they walked towards the hotel. Unlike Wichita Falls or Coopers Ridge, no one stopped to chat. People hurried towards whatever they were doing next or where ever they were going.

It was disappointing in a way. Nora had wanted to speak with others, get a feel for city living and maybe make some new friends. Most ignored her smiles or nods.

"They got some rude people here," Rusty said so loud one of the men passing by stared him down. "It's true," he told the man, staring back.

"Rusty, don't start anything." Nora wanted to get to the hotel in one piece.

He tightened his hold on her and leaned in. "I won't start anything but I hope you don't expect me to be friendly to these people. They run around up and down the street looking like the saddest people in the world. Did you see that man?" He pointed to a fellow in a three-piece suit, who almost ran them over in his hurry to race across the street while it was clear to do so.

"Ignore them, Rusty. They don't have any problem ignoring you." She turned to him. "Let's get to our rooms and then go have some fun."

"Here?" He actually looked shocked. "What the heck are we gonna do here?"

"Well, I'm sure we'll find plenty to keep us busy."

As if on cue, a woman walked toward them holding a stack of papers. She handed one to Nora. "Be sure to come see our production of Hamlet tonight!"

Then she was gone, handing out her advertisements to others walking along the busy street.

"See, Rusty. We can go see Hamlet tonight. Let's have a delicious supper at the hotel dining room and then the theatre. Isn't this wonderful?"

Rusty grumbled before turning to the door of the hotel, holding it open for her. He was trying but the rumbling going on in his chest made her realize this was going to be a lot harder than she originally thought.

Would Rusty hate the city and demand to leave, cutting her visit short?

Or, would he be a good sport and escort her to the places she wanted to see?

Only time will tell, she thought, smiling as they entered the large, brick two-story hotel. No one was going to ruin her adventure!

<> <>

Rusty was getting worried. The city was bustling with all kinds of chaos. He was more laid back than the people here. How in the world was he going to keep Nora happy, become her suitor and keep up with all the new things Dallas society had to offer?

As they secured a key and followed the bellboy up the wide stairway to the second floor, Nora seemed rather quiet herself. Had she changed her mind? Maybe she'd tell him to load up the wagon, they were leaving before they settled in and that suited him fine! He wasn't liking this place one bit.When she checked her room number and turned to him, her eyes bright with excitement, he knew then this was the beginning of a grand adventure. Rusty was determined to keep that look on her face.

He grinned.

It may not have been what he wanted to do but if Nora wanted a grand adventure, by George, she was going to get one!

After a leisurely afternoon of rest, Rusty decided he better wash up and put on his fancy suit, as he liked to call the outfit. He stared in the oval mirror above the wash stand, realizing how out of place he looked. Jeez, bristles stuck out on his scruffy face and he had sun burnt skin from too many hours on the range.

Sometimes Rusty liked putting his face in the wind, no wide brim to cover his eyes. He knew Nora did too. They'd often ride like that more towards evening when the sun laid low after all the work was done. But you can tell he was a hard-working man who took his job seriously. He didn't know if that mattered to someone when they were being courted. Was he too ugly to court Nora?

What he'd give to be out on the range right now instead of getting all fancied up for a dinner they probably didn't even want to be at. He shook himself. No use getting riled. If Nora wanted flamboyant then he'd give her whatever her heart desired.

Slipping through the door, he walked past hers and stopped for a moment, careful not to make any noise to disturb her in case she was resting. There was no sound coming from inside so he figured he'd have time before he had to fetch her for their meal. This might be fun after all, he thought, as he took the stairs two at a time.

At the front desk a young man greeted him. "Hello, I'm Donald Howe. How may I help you, sir, er, Mr. Rivers?"

"Can you direct me to the nearest barber?"

Mr. Howe stared at the red clump of hair smashed down on Rusty's head. "Oh, absolutely. Take a right out the door, three blocks down you will see the shop in big white letters on the window."

"Thank you." Rusty didn't waste any time heading towards the barber shop. Dallas was a busy town with way too many people. He hoped there wasn't a line outside the barber shop. He didn't want to dally too long and miss supper with his bride-to-be."

At least that's how he looked at things. She kind of told him she'd marry him after they went on this adventure, so he was going to do everything in his power to give her the best time in Dallas she ever had. Including making himself look presentable.

Rusty glanced towards the Trinity River. It ran all along the outskirts of the city. A storm was once again brewing which may cause the river to flood some areas. He hoped Dallas wasn't one of those places when the river decided to let loose.

He stepped inside, glad to see it was almost empty. A man a few years older than himself was on the barber chair, his cheeks and chin lathered up. Rusty took off his hat, placing it carefully on the peg by the door. He sat down to wait his turn.

The barber turned to acknowledge him. "Howdy, sir. I'll be with you in about five minutes. What'll you have?"

"I think a trim and a shave will be in order," Rusty told him. The man in the chair seemed to be sleeping. His eyes were closed, his chest rising now and again.

"Well, I'll be happy to. My names John, I'm the only barber so far on Main Street. Guess that'll be changing soon since the city is growing like crazy. Your first time in the city?"

"Yep, name's Rusty. Rusty Rivers."

"A pleasure to meet you." The man went on and on, he wasn't going to quiet down too quickly. Rusty's ears were starting to ache from all the noise. He sighed, twiddling his thumbs as he leaned back. Five minutes was long past and the barber was still going on and on.

"Are you here for work or pleasure, Mr. Rivers."

"Call me Rusty. We're here on a grand adventure for the lady I love." There he said it, claimed her out loud. It sounded so silly, even to his own ears but he didn't care. Nora was all that was important even if the barber made fun of him.

Rusty was surprised when the barber didn't laugh.

"A grand adventure? What are you planning to see? Why, there's so much to see and do in our beautiful city."

"I wouldn't call it beautiful!" The man in the chair interrupted and blinked as if he woke up in that instant. "Are you done with me yet?"

The barber finished wiping his face and took off the cloth from around his neck. "There you are, sir. It has been an honor to serve you, Mr. Fields."

The man paid for his shave, stopping by where Rusty sat on the padded chair. "I am assuming you will be taking your lady to the Opera House this evening for the production of Hamlet?"

Rusty stood. "How in the world did you know?" He narrowed his eyes at the man.

The stranger laughed. "I have my actors staked out at the livery, the rail road station and the river handing out flyers. My name is Thomas Field, I own Field's Opera House."

Rusty stared at the man, waiting for him to continue or head out the door. He had a haircut and shave to get done before supper. "Howdy," was all he said.

Mr. Fields held out his hand. Rusty reluctantly shook hands, not sure where this conversation was going.

He went to step away when Fields placed a hand on his shoulder. "I can read people fairly well, it's how I find my actors for the stage. It seems to me like you may need some help with this grand adventure you're on."

Rusty didn't know if he should trust a complete stranger. He glanced at the barber who stood waiting beside the chair holding a towel. He flung a hand through a clump of hair. "I need to get my hair cut and shave before supper."

Mr. Fields nodded. "I understand your reluctance to let a total stranger help. I guarantee after this evening, you will no longer feel this way." He reached in his vest pocket to hand him a small card.

"Please accept this. When the show is over, here are directions to my private residence. Tonight is the last show and we always have a post party for selective individuals. This card will also give you entrance. Your lady will be so impressed she'll fall madly in love and more. There will be quite the crowd tonight."

Rusty took the card. How about that! He grinned and shook the man's hand again. "Why, thanks. We'll try to be there. Not familiar with the address on here though."

"Don't worry, when you leave the Theatre ask for directions and show this card. The attendant will know where to send you."

"Very good. Now I must have my shave before my lady gets tired of waiting for me." Rusty almost laughed at himself. He was sounding quite the dandy.

On the way back, Rusty stopped by several merchants who had their wares sitting outside their stores. He looked over several carts filled with kitchen wares and jewellery to other trinkets. After selecting a few items, he made his way back to the hotel to collect the woman he loved.

<> <>

It was soon time for supper and Nora had overslept. When she had retired to this room earlier, the bed looked so tempting she had only wanted to rest for a few minutes. That wound up to be hours.

Now she was hurrying like a senseless young girl, trying to get ready for her handsome suitor.

The only dress suitable for a night out watching a play was her wedding dress she had kept over the years. She purposely brought it along with her in case she needed more than the cotton dress and skirts she wore.

Standing in front of the mirror, Nora didn't feel nostalgic at all thinking about the day she wore it to marry Robert. Her heart had been broken and there was no turning back. She wanted to remember the good times but their life together had been hard work. In the beginning, he was kind and gentle and she'd cherish those memories. But now, she wanted to move on and make a new life for herself and the White Ranch.

Her dead husband had already been wiped from her mind. As far as Nora was concerned, it was here and now that mattered. This dress now represented a new way of life for her. She was going to wear it not only tonight but on her wedding day as well.

Her wedding to Rusty.

Because even though she wanted a grand adventure, she wanted a life with him more. It hadn't taken her all but five minutes after reaching the city to figure this out. But it didn't hurt a girl to have a little fun in the meantime. Plus, she told him they had to each try a few new things out first before making a decision.

It mattered to Nora that this time things would be done right.

She hoped he would ask her again to marry him. What if he didn't ask her again?

What if, after spending time with her, Rusty decides he doesn't want to marry her after all? What if he goes out in the city alone and finds someone else? Was this a chance she was willing to take?

She had to do this, to make sure Rusty would never change his mind and want someone else, like her husband had.

Not that Rusty was even close to Robert in character. He was the exact opposite.

He wasn't going to get away from her.

No way.

What she was doing was for their own good. Then they'd both be certain they wanted each other. Robert's infidelity had turned her into a woman who was afraid to trust.

And she trusted Rusty with her life.

But maybe not her heart.

It was hard to let go and love someone new.

Even though she'd known Rusty for a lifetime.

A loud knock shattered her thoughts. Nora smiled at the image in the mirror. Her hair turned out perfect. She gave herself one last look before heading towards the constant knocking.

For a suitor, the man was so impatient!

Chapter 5

Nora smiled when Rusty's mouth dropped open.

"You best shut that jaw else you'll be drooling all over your shirt collar!"

"My Lord above, Nora, you are as beautiful as the day is long."

Rusty stood there in the door way holding a small bouquet of pink and white flowers. The knuckles on his fist were white. "Thank you for the compliment, Rusty. You are about to crush the stems if you don't hand them over!"

He actually looked embarrassed. Gazing down at his hands, he loosened the grip causing the whole bouquet to slip from his hands. "Dog gone it now look at what I did!"

Rusty and Nora bent over at the exact same time to pick up the bouquet and bumped heads. "Oh, dear!"

Rusty took hold of her arms and held her out in front of him, studying her face to make sure he didn't hurt her. "I am so sorry, Nora, this isn't starting out good at all."

She laughed at the sheer panic on his face. Then she wrapped her arms around his neck and gave him a hug. "You are doing fine, Rusty. We both are a bit nervous and not good at this courtship stuff at all. Why don't we just forget the formal stuff and act like ourselves."

"Well, I thought I was."

Then he laughed. Like the old Rusty she'd known so well, not this stiff-necked man in a suit trying to impress her.

She laughed too. "Mr. Rusty Rivers, you clean up mighty fine." He wore a black wool double-breasted frock coat that stopped at his thighs and a pair of walnut canvas trousers. His beard was neatly trimmed and those red tresses she loved so much were neatly cut. It was almost too much. She actually preferred the scattered Rusty look but this was nice, too. The fact was he was trying to impress her.

Didn't he know he already had?

"Let me have those flowers, Rusty." He handed them over, the bouquet looking rather shabby with some of the pink petals lying on the floor.

"I'm sorry they are a mess."

"Oh, Rusty, they are beautiful. I'll place them in this jar on the dresser." After adding some water from the pitcher, she took one of the pretty pink flowers from the bunch and looked in the mirror, careful to place it in her hair.

She turned.

Rusty was staring at her open mouthed again.

"I'm ready to go to supper."

It took him a moment to move, then he held out his arm and opened the door at the same time she reached for it. Fumbling around, they actually made it through the door and down the stairs without incident.

An attendant stood at the entrance to the hotel's restaurant, offering to seat them. There was quite a bit of activity this time of day as everyone who stayed at the hotel seemed to be in the dining room for supper.

Nora and Rusty were placed along the wall in a quiet area of the room, away from the center of attention. She was glad they wouldn't be dead in the middle of all the activity. Even though she was so excited for the play, she wasn't used to all the noise.

After they ordered, Rusty reached across and took her hand. "Nora, I know you are wanting a grand adventure and I'm going to make sure your evening is exquisite."

Nora tilted her head, watching Rusty as he struggled to please her. He seemed uncomfortable. "Are you having second thoughts about escorting me to the Opera House tonight, Rusty? If so, no need to worry, we won't have to stay long. I'd like to see what it entails."

He shook his head and patted her hand. "I'm fine, Nora. Don't worry about me. Although, I do have a surprise for you."

She looked down to see his hand over hers. It felt nice and seemed right. When he mentioned a surprise, she perked up. Maybe he seemed a bit nervous but that didn't mean Rusty wasn't trying. Perhaps she needed to stop worrying about him. "A surprise? For me, Rusty? What is the surprise?"

She lifted a hand to the flower in her hair. He had already given her a gift. Yet, she was curious what else he had in store.

Rusty reached into the pocket of his wool coat. "I thought of you when I saw this."

He handed her a gold pin with a beautifully carved horse made out of a fine silver. It was perfect for her riding outfit but she was wearing it tonight to go to the Opera House. "Would you help me?" she asked.

He seemed surprised. "You're putting it on now?"

"Of course, why wouldn't I wear such a wonderful gift?"

Rusty looked around first before pushing his chair back. He gave her a hand, pinning it to the high part of her collar. He stood back and nodded. "Beautiful."

She smiled. "You do have good taste in gifts."

Rusty bowed then sat back down, grinning. "I meant you."

She actually blushed. Nora had thought she was too old to do so but once again she was proven wrong. This journey she was on was proving to be somewhat exhausting and yet exhilarating at the same time.

As they ate supper, Nora realized Rusty was going along with the motions of escorting her but in reality he probably would be even happier to sit here and talk the rest of the night.

If she was to be honest with herself, she'd rather enjoy a cup of coffee and talk, too.

Why did she have to go to the Opera?

She didn't. But, because she set this in motion, Nora wanted to see it through. A woman deserved to be pampered and escorted around this big city. Even if she was having second thoughts and was dying to get back to the ranch. She wanted to at least give it a day and see a play to boot.

"Nora, you deaf?"

"I'm not deaf. Are you? Maybe I answered and you didn't hear me."

"I've been watching that pretty mouth of yours and it ain't moved since I spoke to you."

She dropped the napkin on her now empty plate. The moment she did so, one of the staff took it away. "Okay, I admit I was wool-gathering about the play tonight, so no, I did not hear you."

"We should probably get going."

"Yes."

Rusty didn't make an effort to leave the table.

"Rusty? What else do you have up your sleeve?"

He smiled, his left cheek twitching. "I guess you do know me more than anyone else, Nora. I was going to wait until later to tell you but I can't."

"Oh? Tell me what?" She was curious now. Rusty didn't ever get excited about anything unless it had to do with the ranch.

He opened his coat and pulled out a card. "Take a look at this."

Nora read the invitation from top to bottom. Confused, she read it again. "Rusty, how did you get this?"

He shrugged. "I guess I know people of importance."

Nora didn't say anything for a moment and then she grinned. "I guess it don't matter how you got this but I am impressed, Rusty Rivers. You have done well."

Rusty helped her with her chair. "You leave it to me, Nora. I'll show you the best time of your life, in this city or at home. Where ever you go, I'm going to be there with you and for you."

Nora turned to him as they went to leave. "Rusty, what a romantic thing to say."

"And I can be romantic, too."

They stood in front of the hotel, her arm tucked into his. When Rusty turned, she lifted her face to him. He looked so serious all of a sudden. Nora wasn't sure but it looked as if he may try to kiss her.

"Rusty?"

He didn't say a word, but splayed his fingers across her cheek. "You are my life, Nora White."

She almost swooned as he dipped his head and kissed her so softly at first she wasn't sure if he actually did so. As her eyelids fluttered shut, his kiss deepened, and she felt herself move forward into his arms. It was their first real kiss and it was perfect.

"Are you planning on going to see the show?" a voice asked, interrupting them. Nora and Rusty both stepped away at the same time. A tall, friendly looking man with freckles across his face and a rather large stove-pipe hat stood there with a crooked smile. "I can escort you both to the show if you'd like?"

Nora was the first to recover. "Of course."

As they made their way down the boarded side walk, Nora noticed several others were also being escorted to the show. The theatre group was all over the city tonight making sure to bring people in to see the play.

The memory of Rusty's kiss was still on her lips. She turned to see how he was faring. He appeared normal except for the fact he was way too quiet. She gathered it had him in a dander, too. They had never kissed this way before. A peck on the cheek here and there, a hug like old friends but never, ever a kiss that shot fire in between her toes!

Nora sighed with relief when he finally turned to give her a big smile. "Let's enjoy the show," he said before buying their tickets at the box office. They found some seats about halfway through the theatre. Thick curtains covered most of the stage while the sound of footsteps were heard behind it.

Excitement tore through Nora. This was the first time she was ever in a theatre. The room was lavish, with oil lamps flickering all along the fancy dark wooded walls. Their seats were cushioned and soft, the intricate detail of the wood carved throughout its frame. Nora honestly felt as if she were royalty.

Rusty took her hand, holding it gently in his own. She gazed over to give him a smile and caught him watching her. All she was able to do was smile back, remembering how his mouth felt on hers.

The moment the show started, the lights were doused, leaving only a few flickering lamps that cast shadows over the crowd. The whole room quieted as they waited in anticipation for the curtains to be drawn.

Nora wasn't disappointed. The whole show was a hit. She clapped along with the others as the lights came back on in full force.

Rusty grunted. "That wasn't as bad as I thought it would be."

"No?"

He stood, holding out a hand to help her up. "How like you this play?" he teased, using Hamlets own words.

"Me thinks you tease too much, sir." Nora told him, taking his hand as they made their way out of the theatre. She waited while Rusty stopped to ask directions to the Field's post-theatre party. When he showed an employee his card, they pointed and gave directions.

"You'll know the moment you get there. You can't miss the house, it takes up the size of a city block."

Rusty and Nora began to walk away from the center of the city towards the residential district. It appeared as if others were walking to the Field homestead so they fell in behind a small crowd that left the theatre the same time they did.

"The man who gave us directions was right. Take a look at this place!"

Nora didn't know where the house stopped or started. It appeared out of nowhere, candles lit in the windows, an iron gated fence keeping trespassers out except for the large open gate where a tall man in a black suit stood checking each persons card.

Nora and Rusty made their way inside. "I feel as if I am surrounded by royalty. I am not dressed for this type of posh entertainment."

Rusty tried to reassure her. "Nora, you look beautiful. These fancy ladies can't hold a candle to you."

She blushed. It was a sweet thing for Rusty to say but Nora was truthful to herself if nothing else. Her plain looks didn't compare to these flamboyant women who wore tons of jewels and tiara's that sparkled in the candle light. She wore a simple gown of cream color with her hair in a braided bun and a flower attached.

Rusty turned her to him, clasping his hands on her shoulders. She had no other choice but to look into his eyes. They sparkled with merriment. "Nora White, are you here to have a grand adventure?"

She nodded. "Of course I am."

"Well, then. Let's have a glass of champagne and enjoy the entertainment. I'll be right here if you need me."

He was right. She was here to have fun. She had asked for this and now it was here in front of her to enjoy. Why not?

Throwing her shoulders back, she picked up a glass of champagne when a waiter held out a tray. Rusty refused. "I'd rather have a whiskey," he complained.

"Oh, come now, Rusty. You must live this grand adventure with me." Before the waiter walked away she picked up another glass and handed it to him.

He took it reluctantly, sniffing the liquid and wrinkling his nose. "Stuff always made my nose itch."

"You don't sniff it, Rusty, drink it." She laughed softly when she went to take a sip and it actually did make her nose twitch, too.

"I told you," he said, puffing out his chest and laughing out loud.

It wasn't long until most of the cast members showed up at the party, bringing along the merriment and camaraderie that went along with a troupe of actors.

Rusty and Nora stood on the sidelines talking and watching. It was nice to sip their champagne and laugh. A few others introduced themselves but the majority of wealthy attendees stayed in small circles amongst themselves. Nora didn't mind one bit. She had no desire to mingle with others who looked at her with disdain. Was it her gown? She didn't much care. Nora was having fun.

Rusty hiccuped, causing Nora to laugh out loud. A few heads turned while some frowns appeared before turning away. "I suppose we aren't quite as dignified as this crowd," Nora told him.

He smiled, taking another sip while pointing his pinky in the air. "To be or not to be, this is the question," he mimicked.

"Oh, Rusty, you make me laugh," she told him. "I'll bet you memorized those two lines while sitting in the theatre bored with the play."

"You got me there, Nora. It was nice and all to see you enjoy yourself though."

She balanced the empty champagne glass in her hand. "I have to be honest here. I enjoyed sitting with you in the theatre and watching all the characters but I had no clue what they were talking about either."

She watched his shoulders relax at her confession.

"I'm relieved to hear it because I wasn't sure what we'd talk about during our evening rides on the range. I can't quote Shakespeare. I can quote cowboy though. Howdy, Ma'am," he said and tipped his hat.

Nora flung her head back and laughed out loud, drawing attention from a small theatre group that happened to be standing in a small circle across the room. One of the actresses turned her head and her eyes widened when she saw Rusty standing there.

"Rusty! Oh, Rusty!" She waved and excused herself, hurrying across the room. "Oh my goodness, is it really you!"

Rusty sucked in a deep breath. Nora saw him stiffen and then hold open his arms. He took a few steps forward. She wrapped her arms around his neck in a familiar way.

Nora looked around for another waiter. As if he read her thoughts, one appeared with a tray filled with full goblets. Nora snatched one from the oval tray and gulped it down like water.

After what seemed like hours even though it was mere seconds, Rusty motioned her over. "Nora, meet Millie Omaha. We grew up in the same town. She ran off to become a vaudeville star!"

Nora gave a polite nod and smile, uncertain if this woman was a friend of Rusty or much more. He seemed shocked when she first recognized him.

"Why don't you come meet my friends?" she told him, looking at Nora in a friendly way. The woman tried to include Nora and she was grateful.

She refused. "I want to try some sweets at the food table," Nora told them. "You go on, Rusty, enjoy time with your old friend."

Rusty looked confused. He shook his head. "If you aren't coming, then I'll stay with you," he told her.

Nora held up her hand, giving him one of her down to business looks. "It's fine, Rusty, really. I want you to enjoy yourself."

Rusty watched her with guarded eyes then turned to Millie. He took her arm as she led the way to her group of friends. Nora had to grin when he looked back several times, making a face at her. She waved him away, shaking her head.

A stab of fear did go through her belly when she saw the other woman hug Rusty. She had explained to him before they came to Dallas that they should both experiment and go out and about themselves to make sure there was no one else out there they wanted. Because of her fears from Robert cheating, she had made it clear to Rusty this had to happen. Now it fell in her lap without even realizing.

Was this a test?

Was this woman from his past placed here to test his feelings for Nora?

She stood at the lavish food table, not realizing she had stacked several cakes on her plate, one on top of the other.

"Are you going to eat them all by yourself?" A man's deep voice asked.

She set the plate down, filled with embarrassment. "Oh, my, I was lolly-gagging, wasn't I?" When she looked up the man standing at her with a bright smile took her breath away. She had never seen such a handsome man before.

Rusty, her beloved, was not the most handsome man in the world but she loved the way his hair flopped in such a way and how his deep, intense eyes watched her. She loved his whiskers even when he didn't trim them. She loved everything about Rusty but this man was so handsome she wondered how he kept himself so immaculate. Dark hair neatly groomed, a set of white teeth that seemed to sparkle and his face was so perfectly shaped.

Other women in the room were drawn to him the moment he appeared at her side. She glanced over her shoulder to see a few ladies whisper while staring right at her.

She didn't particularly care for jealousy so she moved closer to him and laughed before extending her hand. "I'm pleased to meet you. My name is Nora White."

"Nora White, it is solely my pleasure," he said, lifting her hand to his mouth and placing a soft, slow kiss there. He never did tell her his name.

It did nothing for her but she looked to see the ladies watching closely. Nora was having fun or maybe the champagne was making her head a little bubbly. She looked over to where Rusty was standing among the small crowd of actors. His friend Millie was awful close, hanging on to his every word and brushing up against his arm now and again. Nora gritted her teeth without realizing.

The stranger followed her line of vision. "Ah, now I understand what is going on. If I may help you, I am a lover of all things entertaining, my dear. I'd love to help you make your suitor envious."

Nora shook her head. "Oh, no, I don't like that type of behavior and would not want to be the cause of any stress upon Rusty."

"Rusty? Well, it looks as if he is enjoying himself. Now, let me help you. Shall we dance?"

Before Nora realized what was happening, the tall handsome man swung her across the room as the orchestra struck up a lively song. Dear Lord in heaven, Nora had no idea how to dance!

Chapter 6

Rusty reached for his hip but the holster he usually wore was no longer there. It was back at the hotel and probably a good thing. He narrowed his eyes at the tall dark-haired man swinging Nora around the ballroom like she was a sack of potatoes!

He had to stop this nonsense. Right as he took a step to go clobber the man, a hand brushed across his forearm. "Would you like to dance?" Millie asked.

He sighed. It wouldn't hurt to calm down before he lost his temper and made a fool of himself. He escorted Millie to the dance floor, inches away from where Nora and the stranger were swaying back and forth. He glared at the back of the man's head.

Nora peeked over the man's shoulder. When she saw Rusty, she frowned, then turned away. All of a sudden her hand went around the strangers neck. What in the world was she thinking!

He stopped dancing. This was too much. "Nora White!"

The music continued on, his voice failing to get her attention.

Millie seemed concerned. "Rusty?" She stood in front of him. "We're on the dance floor and you stopped, what is the matter?"

Rusty had to pull himself together. This feeling of jealousy ran through his blood like a leech sucking on a man's skin. He began to move his feet and yet still keep an eye on those two. If the man dared to touch her in an inappropriate way, Rusty was going to put a stop to that nonsense.

He was here with Nora. He brought her here and he planned to escort her home. Why, he was her suitor. What was he doing dancing with Millie? Maybe this was all his fault after all.

Rusty's shoulders dropped. He failed. Their night out was turning into a disaster. All he had wanted to do was make Nora happy in this type of environment and he lost her within an hour of being here. She had wanted a grand adventure but by the looks of things it wasn't with him.

Then he remembered their conversation at the crusty line shack. She had told him they needed to go out on the town alone to make sure they wanted each other. Rusty was certain she had said it because of Robert. Her dead husband had hurt her terribly. Didn't she know he would never do that to her? He saw how hard it had been all those years for Nora, the nights she spent alone crying on her porch. He had even held her in his arms at times, reassuring her things would get better and they had.

Then he realized he was no better than Robert because here he stood with another lady in his arms dancing around because he had been jealous of her dancing with a stranger.

Rusty had to explain himself. He didn't want Nora to misunderstand his intentions. As the music stopped playing, couples left the dance floor. Rusty thanked Millie for the dance. "I have to escort Nora home," he told her, making excuses to get away.

"Of course," Millie smiled at him. "It was so nice to see you again after all these years. If you'd like, our group is planning a day in the park with a picnic lunch and all. We are going to sing a few songs to the public as a thank you for coming to our play."

Just as Rusty started to refuse, Nora and the stranger appeared. "Oh, Rusty that sounds like a wonderful idea. I'll be busy tomorrow as Miguel has invited me on a carriage ride through the park. You must go and enjoy yourself."

Rusty turned to Nora, frowning. "Miguel?"

Miguel bowed. "I am at your service. Miguel Castinova." The man was a charmer, Rusty knew that right away but he shook hands to be polite. He'd rather wrap his hands around his neck and choke the daylights out of the man. He shook himself, was trying to rid himself of such evil thoughts. But they were lurking in the back of his mind as the four talked for over an hour.

Nora kept glancing over at him but Rusty was determined to stay back and allow her some space to enjoy the evening. He had failed as a romantic suitor. If he hadn't been attending to her more, instead of meeting Millie's friends, Nora would be laughing and clinging onto his every word. Instead, she was enticed by a dark-haired gentleman who probably had so much more than Rusty would ever have. Nora deserved much more.

She deserved someone who would make her happy and right now all Rusty noticed was how she smiled and laughed at everything Miguel said.

He felt as if he had been punched in the gut. Nora wanted to enjoy her grand adventure so much. It was his presence that would eventually hold her back. Because the two of them were always together on the ranch didn't mean she'd be happy with him forever. Had he been kidding himself?

"Rusty?" Millie laid a hand on his arm.

Now she was encouraging him to go to the park with Millie for a picnic. Did Nora want him out of the way so she may pursue a courtship with this Miguel man? He took a step back.

"Millie, I'll meet you at the park tomorrow at noon. Now, if you will excuse me, I need to get some fresh air." He turned to Nora. "I'll be outside on the bench I saw near the front gate. When you are ready to leave, I'll escort you back to the hotel." He tipped his hat and didn't wait for an answer.

Rusty had enough of this evening. He found the bench empty and was glad for that at least. He was done talking for the night. All he wanted to do was go to the hotel, pack his things and head back to the ranch. Where he belonged.

Except tomorrow he had to go to a park and pretend to be enjoying a picnic lunch with a woman he knew from many years ago. They were childhood friends, nothing more. He had no feelings for her whatsoever.

Did Nora think he had feelings for Millie? Now that he was away from the situation he was starting to realize Nora had watched him carefully all evening. If she was so enamored by the tall, handsome Miguel she wouldn't be eyeing him up and down, that's for sure.

Rusty sat back and smiled as it dawned on him. She had been jealous of him speaking with Millie! The way Millie tugged at his sleeve was enough to make anyone jealous. Why hadn't he seen this from the beginning?

Some days Rusty felt old and clueless. He wasn't a city slicker like the man Nora danced with. Yet, Nora's eyes had been on him and not Miguel.

He wanted to find her and take her in his arms and sweep her away from all the luxurious and charming atmosphere this very moment. He knew in his heart Nora would give it all up for her horses and ranch.

That included Rusty, too!

He was an idiot!

But, he'd give her time to enjoy her evening and wait here. Rusty sat back, relaxed now, knowing his Nora would come to him when she tired of the gala event and allow him to escort her home.

It wasn't long.

A soft voice and a warm breath of air brushed across his shoulder. "Rusty? May I sit with you?"

He slid over, making room for her to sit alongside him. He placed a hand over hers, like he always did. "Did you enjoy your evening?"

"It was nice. I enjoyed it more when you were inside."

Rusty leaned back and closed his eyes, revelling in the fact she was beside him. "I needed fresh air. It's much better outside."

Even though he couldn't see her face, he knew she was smiling when she spoke. "You do like your wide open spaces."

"Hmm, as do you."

She nodded. "Yes, I certainly do. I'm picturing us riding across the South Range, racing towards that big cluster of oak trees along the banks of the creek."

He smiled. Here they were, sitting on a bench at the entrance to one of the most posh homes in Dallas, reminiscing about their own home. All the glitz and glamor didn't come close to what they had at the ranch. Nora was one in a million, she didn't go for all that fancy stuff. He knew that even when he was fuming earlier with blind jealousy. He had no plans to let her fall in love with a city slicker.

"I need you to know I didn't plan on going to the park with Millie tomorrow until you insisted I go. We are childhood friends, that's all."

"I had to be sure, Rusty. You remember what I said, don't you? We both must go out and about to make sure we are the right one for each other."

He nodded, his eyes still closed. It was nice talking to her like this. It was almost like being at home, sitting on the front porch in the evening. Except he knew when he opened his eyes all he'd see is the big city staring him in the face. "I'll go through the motions, Nora, if that's what is required of me. You're the one for me. Always were. Always will be. I don't understand why you don't see this."

His words were not clipped. They were honest and how he truly felt. If she didn't understand this, then maybe she wasn't ready to spend the rest of their lives together. Maybe all he was to her was a ranch hand, one of the guys that made her life run smooth. Was that how she felt about him? He doubted it but maybe he needed to bring it to her attention.

"It is because of Robert. I have to know, Rusty."

He let go of her hand and turned to her, his eyes wide open now. "What is it you have to know? That my love for you is pure and raw and all I want to do is keep you safe and with me all the days of my life? Do you want to know that when I saw you with Miguel I wanted to place my hands around his throat and strangle him because he looked at you? I had plans to marry you right in this city, Nora, before we leave because I don't want anyone else to have you. What do you want me to say, Nora? I love you."

A tear splashed on his hand. He raised his eyes to her face to see her crumple in front of him. "Oh, Rusty. I love you, too. I truly do. But I still think this will be good for us, just to make sure. What if you regret marrying me? What if you go on this picnic tomorrow and find you have a common interest with Millie? All you know is me. What if you want more?"

Rusty took a deep breath. "I don't want more, Nora. All I want is you."

She swiped at a fallen tear. "I do understand. Robert swore I was his true love. He told me every single night before we turned in that he loved me. I believed him. Even after he cheated on me with the widow that one time, he spoke of his undying love. And, the truth is I believed him because I wanted to make my marriage work. Turns out it was all a scam. I'm still trying to figure it all out, Rusty."

He did understand. Truth be told, Rusty didn't deserve this wonderful lady. She had been through a lifetime of deceit. He had to be honest with her. "Nora, I'm going to tell you something and I am not saying this because I want to hurt you. I'm telling you because I don't ever want you to find out I didn't tell you everything I knew about Robert's shenanigans."

"What are you saying?"

Rusty ran his thumb back and forth across her hand. "Robert lied to you over and over. He had a problem, Nora. It wasn't you. He didn't stop with that one time. Even after he confessed his affair, he continued to go see Widow Young. I don't believe she was in agreement. I heard some things you may not want to hear but I have to tell you so the hatred for the widow stops."

"Hatred? She slept with my husband right in front of my nose."

Rusty shook his head. "I'm not totally convinced she ever agreed."

"What!"

"One of their farm hands told one of our men Robert had been forcing her. He overheard it several times in their barn and other places. She didn't have a choice. Robert threatened her with taking the twins from her. She didn't think she had a choice."

Nora gasped. "Oh, dear Lord above!"

Rusty almost regretted telling her. Yet, he knew if he didn't, it would always be between them. Her hand went to her face. "I slapped that woman hard across the face! I need to speak with her, Rusty."

"In good time. I think you need to digest all of this before we go running off to see the Widow Young."

Nora sighed beside him. "You are right. I want to go home."

"Home? As in back to our hotel?"

She shook her head. "No, Rusty. I want to go home. This is all nice and all and fun but my heart belongs on the ranch."

"We have dates tomorrow."

"Thanks to me. Can we cancel?" She stood up.

Rusty sat on the bench staring up at the most beautiful woman in the world. As he did so, he noticed how the stars dotted the night sky. He slid off the bench and dropped to one knee. Rusty took her hand. "Nora White, may I have the honor of marrying you?"

She stared up at the starry night for the longest time. He waited, unable to see her face in the dark, even with the translucent candles dotting the gardens. Her shoulders shook. He wasn't sure if Nora was laughing or crying. "Oh, Rusty, you pick the worst time and place to ask a girl to marry you."

He looked around as several of the fancy ladies came outside, being escorted down the walk. "Does it matter where we are, Nora?"

She looked him in the eye then. "I guess it doesn't. But it does matter where we get married. Yes, Rusty Rivers, I will marry you."

He stood and gathered her in his arms, placing small kisses along her jaw line and cheek. His mouth drifted across hers, pressing his lips to hers. It was a deep, meaningful moment, one he would cherish forever. It was the day Nora White finally said yes.

Chapter 7

"Rusty, you have to go."

"Nora, I can't go now that I'm an engaged man. I have a fiancé."

They were having breakfast in the hotel restaurant. Nora was not going to let him go back on his promise. "You told Millie you would join her for a picnic and you have to keep your word. Just as I told Miguel the same. We are going."

She dared Rusty to argue with her. Of course, in Rusty style, he did. Setting his fork down and taking a big gulp of the strong coffee, he stared her in the face like a man with a crazy idea. "I think we should saddle up and ride out of town right now!"

She laughed. "Rusty, that is so rude of you to even suggest we run out on our promise. We can't. It would not be right." And yet, she wanted to do just that. Nora had wanted some excitement in her life. What if she turned and ran?

The thought was brewing in her brain as she finished her coffee. Until she saw Miguel, standing in the doorway, looking around for her. He waved when he saw her. "Oh, dear. I was seriously contemplating your idea, Rusty. But, it's too late. Here's Miguel."

Rusty leaned in to the table. "We can run now. Let him chase us down the street. He won't be able to catch up, look at that dandy! I'll bet he ain't got no muscles under that fancy shirt he wears."

Nora still had a smile on her face when she turned to Miguel. He picked up her hand and leaned in for a kiss. "Miss White, I am here to escort you on a delightful, romantic carriage ride."

When he lifted his face, he slyly gazed at Rusty before he gave her a devilish smile. He was still in his actor mode, trying to make Rusty jealous to get a rise out of him. It had been in good fun last night since Miguel was not interested in courting her. He claimed to be practising his dramatic skills for the theatre. Nora was shocked she went along with his plan but the fact was she was so jealous of Millie, she had agreed.

She disliked jealousy in others and then she went and let it happen to her own self. It was not a trait she admired at all. "Miguel, I appreciate you taking me on a carriage ride today. I must inform you that last night Rusty here asked for my hand in marriage."

Miguel slapped a hand to his face. "Oh, how intriguing. So our plan worked?"

Nora wanted to tell Rusty before he found out like this. She gave him a worried look but he was grinning like crazy. "Plan? What plan?" he asked, but he already figured it out.

Nora threw her napkin on the table. "I think you already know we were pretending to like each other to make you jealous."

Rusty slid his chair back. "I guess that means we can forget the picnic and be on our way."

Nora shook her head. "Oh, no you don't. We are going to honor our plans today, Rusty."

Miguel cleared his throat. "If I may suggest a solution I would be honored to go to the park to meet Millie in your place."

"That's kind of you but haven't you already rented a carriage for our ride today?"

"Yes, and now that our plans have changed, the carriage is at your service for the next few hours. Enjoy a ride around the city with your fiancé." He bowed and disappeared as if he hadn't really been there.

"Well now, this is quite the turn of events."

"A carriage ride? What do we want to do that for? Jeez, Nora, we'll be riding for the next four hours or so to get back to the ranch."

Nora placed her hands on her hips. "Rusty! This is my adventure and we are going on a carriage ride around the city."

"Over my dead body! I ain't gonna be out there for every Tom, Dick and Harry to stare me down riding around like a fancy man!"

Ten minutes later the two were being carted down Main Street in a Prairie Concord buggy with leather seats and dash, led by a beautiful white horse. The driver wore a neat, black suit with matching boots and hat.

Small children turned to stare at the buggy with a white horse. A few small children clapped their hands, staring at the pretty ribbons the carriage company strewn through the horse's mane. Nora watched Rusty's face as he gritted his teeth. He sure didn't like to be put on display but she wasn't going to refuse a wonderful ride through the city.

Once they turned from Main Street towards the river, Rusty calmed down. He had been clutching his fists together for the last ten minutes. Nora leaned towards him, whispering in his ear so the driver didn't hear. "This is so romantic, Rusty."

His jaw slackened a bit when she snuggled up to him. In another second, his arm was around her shoulder. "This is nice," he admitted. "Now that we are away from prodding eyeballs."

"I tend to agree. The river is a nice change of pace." They rode along for some time, watching as a slow moving barge stopped to load up passengers and supplies to take them across the Trinity.

"This is a nice place to have a picnic of our own," Nora said out of the blue.

The moment she spoke the words, the buggy came to a stop.

The driver turned and tipped his hat. "Forgive me for interrupting but I overhead your words. There is a basket and blanket on the bench here overflowing with food. If you would like I can set up a picnic area right under the shaded tree down yonder."

Nora looked at Rusty. "Shall we?"

He nodded. "Why not? If it is here, we may as well eat. Was Miguel going to bring you down here to woo you, Nora?"

She laughed, nodding to the driver to carry on and set them up. "It no longer matters, now, does it? We get to enjoy the afternoon at the river."

The carriage driver escorted them to the shade tree. He placed the blanket on the ground and set the basket in the corner. "I'll be back in approximately one hour," he told them.

Rusty sat on the corner of the blanket while Nora dug in to see what food was in the basket.

He watched the driver take off in the carriage. "The carriage driver is leaving? He said he'd come back in one hour! Was this what Miguel had planned? He wanted to be alone with you here by the river?"

Nora shook her head. Rusty was still jealous of Miguel. "If Miguel had plans for anything inappropriate I would not have stood for it, you should know that. But, don't worry, Rusty, the driver will be back before you know it. You won't be alone with me for too long!"

"Now, Nora! That is not what I meant. It's just that -"

Nora shook her head and pointed a finger at him. "Rusty Rivers, you stop right now! I know exactly what you meant. You are still harboring jealousy over a man who is probably enjoying the day with his theatre friends. Here, have some food."

Rusty did as told. He took off his hat, ruffling his hair. "I don't know what's gotten into me, Nora. My apologies. He was nice enough to let us have this afternoon and I am enjoying the day with you. I'm sorry, I don't belong here in this city. It aggravates me too much."

"Oh, Rusty, it's fine. It is time to go home but this afternoon is nice."

"I guess we'll head out tomorrow for the ranch."

She agreed. "Yes, let's get a fresh start first thing in the morning."

They spent the remainder of the hour eating and talking. The sound of the flowing water of the river drowned out the noise from the city.

"This is living, ain't it?" Rusty mentioned.

"Yes, it is. I want to get married at the ranch, so if you are thinking of springing a surprise wedding on me tonight, don't."

He smiled. Picked up her hand, leaned in to give her a kiss on the cheek. "I had thought of doing just that but I'd rather stand proud in front of your boys."

Nora dropped her gaze to stare at his hand in hers. "You know, Rusty. Those boys are just as much yours as mine. You helped me raise them. You were always there for me every step of the way. Thank you for a lifetime of caring."

Rusty blushed. Nora tilted her head and smiled. "I do love you, Rusty. More than I ever loved Robert. Thank you for being honest and telling me how horrible of a man he was. Do the boys know about his treatment of Widow Young?"

Rusty shook his head. "No, I kept it to myself."

"I only ask one thing of you."

"Anything for you, my love."

She liked him saying those words. It made her feel as if she meant the world to him. "I ask that you forget what my dead husband did all those years ago. I never want my sons or my grandchildren to know what kind of awful things he was capable of. My sons already know too much about his character and most likely harbor ill feelings. However, I don't want the sins of the father to taunt them."

Rusty nodded. "I promise."

"Thank you. Now, there's our carriage. Are you ready to finish our ride?"

Rusty groaned. "I suppose so. Would you care to take a ride through the park?"

Nora looked up. "Why Rusty, I believe you want to make sure Miguel sees us together."

He shrugged then smiled. "I suppose so."

<> <>

The evening turned out to be so romantic. Rusty tried his hardest to give her a last night to remember. He spent the latter part of the afternoon making sure the hotel set up a quiet table for them to enjoy a late dinner. Rusty even took her for a long walk down Main Street afterwards.

The stores were closed by now except there was a small light burning in one small shop on the corner beside the First Methodist Church. Rusty asked her to wait while he went inside. She gazed at the necklaces in the picture window until he returned a few minutes later. Was he going to buy her a present? He had given her so much. She didn't want him to spend any more money.

"Rusty. I must request you stop buying things for me."

He took her arm, steering her back down the street past the Dallas Hook and Ladder Company and the brick building that was the Sanger Brothers Department Store. "What makes you think I bought you something?" His eyes sparkled when he looked at her.

"Because you went inside that jewelery shop without me. I want you to stop, Rusty. You've bought me enough things in the last few days."

He frowned. "I guess you are right but we have to have a ring for your finger. I want everyone to know you are my bride."

Nora was touched. Perhaps it was time to tell him he was much richer than he realized. He had spent a lot of money in the city these past few days. She knew now was the time to disclose her secret.

She stopped in the middle of the street. "May we sit down somewhere, please. I want to speak to you."

Rusty had a panicked look on his face. "I'm sorry, Nora. If buying a ring upsets you I can take it back. The light is still on." She followed his gaze towards the shop to see the light flickering in the window.

"No, Rusty. Let's take a seat on this bench." They were in Courthouse Square where a few benches were scattered here and there in front of some of the buildings. A few couples were taking a stroll, while a lone man sat on one of the benches.

"Rusty. I am watching you spend money left and right on me the whole time we are in the city. I don't mind gifts. Actually, I love the gifts you bought me. I don't want you to spend all of your hard earned money on me."

Rusty touched her cheek with his hand, running his fingers across her cheek. "I don't mind. I've plenty of money, Nora. I've saved over the years."

"You also loaned me quite a chunk of money when my husband died. Do you remember?"

He nodded. "Yes, and it wasn't a loan. It was a gift. I don't regret doing so."

She took a deep breath. "I tried to pay you back over the years but you refused."

"I still refuse. I told you how I felt the day I gave it to you. A rambler like me found a home after years of wandering from ranch to ranch. It was an investment for me, Nora. For you. Don't insult me by offering to pay it back. We were on the brink of losing every single thing we worked hard for. There was no way I wanted to see you lose the ranch. The boys needed a home. It has been forgotten."

"Thank you, Rusty. That money saved our lives."

Rusty grinned. "Want to know where that money came from? My parents were well off, can you believe this? When they died, I cashed in all their stock in the railroad, split the profits between my siblings and me and headed west. It wasn't as if I was losing something by giving you the money to keep the ranch going, Nora. I want you to understand this."

She took his hands. "I do. Being a widowed woman, it was hard to raise a family. I had to learn the ways of ranching and you taught me most of what I know besides the few things Robert taught me when I insisted on learning. He was never too thrilled at the idea of me knowing as much as him."

"So why are we having this conversation?" Rusty was always to the point. It was what she loved about him.

"Because you have owned a part of the White Ranch for the last ten years."

He blinked. "I, what?"

"You are a lot richer than you realize."

"I am?"

"Yes, Rusty. I had a new deed written up in Wichita Falls back then. I'll show you when we get home."

He guffawed. "I'll be darned!"

"We all own the White Ranch equally. You, me, Luke, Adam and Samuel."

"Not necessarily."

It was Nora's turn to blink. "What do you mean?"

He puffed out his chest. "Seems to me once I marry you, then I'll be the man in charge. I believe I'll own your share by making you my wife."

Nora laughed out loud. "Try that, Rusty Rivers and you'll be buried in the grave next to my departed husband."

He gave her a hug. "I'm joshing with you, Nora. The idea that you had part of the land put in my name so long ago shows me how much you trusted me. I am honored and do not deserve this."

"Of course you do." She stood up. "Now that we have those things out of the way, I'm thinking about the sweets counter I saw in the hotel lobby. Perhaps a late night snack may be in order."

"Well, then, my love, let's get you some sweet confections."

They spent the next ten minutes talking and laughing as they made their way back to the hotel. "Rusty, I never told the boys your name is on the deed."

"It doesn't much matter now, does it? We'll be married and it won't make a big difference."

"You are probably right. Perhaps I'll tell them down the road, but, you know what? I kind of like having my own secret."

Rusty held open the door to the hotel. "If it makes you happy, then I'll keep your secret as long as needed.

Chapter 8

One last look at the big city made Nora smile as the dust from the wheels rose up behind her wagon. Nora was anxious to get back to her ranch. Or, their ranch as it would soon be known. Once they were married, she planned to use Nora White Rivers. She wanted to keep her name, she was proud of all they'd been through over the years. Even if her dead husband was a poor excuse of a man for a husband and human being.

When she first decided to take this journey, she wanted a grand adventure. Because she realized her husband was a cheat and liar, she thought by leaving for awhile to think things through would make her a better person. She even thought getting away would revive her spirit. Nora learned so much in the past few days. Even though she knew what was important, she also learned the grass was not as green on the opposite side of the fence. Her mother had always said so and now she had experienced it for herself.

Grand adventure or not, she was going home. Her life was as grand as she made it as far as Nora was concerned. The ranch was where she belonged. Rusty had been riding behind the wagon, humming a merry tune. She knew the moment he came alongside the wagon. "Are you sad to leave, Nora?" he asked.

"You know the answer to that, Rusty. You just want me to say it aloud."

He took his hat off and slapped it on his thigh, wiping the sweat from his brow with the back of his hand. Placing the hat back on, Rusty leaned down. "I had the hotel restaurant pack us a basket filled with sandwiches and some of those fancy sweets you were stuffing your mouth with last night."

He sure had a way with words. She was so happy to be heading home she didn't reprimand him for his use of language. "That's sweet of you, Rusty. I'd rather go straight home but the horses will have to rest after awhile."

"It's what I figured, too." He nodded to her and fell in behind the wagon, taking up the rear once again. She knew Rusty liked to watch his surroundings. He began to hum a lively tune again, his eyes on the road ahead.

Nora swayed to the sound of his voice. A few hours later, almost on the outskirts of Wichita Falls, there was a lovely waterfall before entering town. Nora pulled the wagon to a stop. "How about here?"

Rusty nodded. They could've gone to Jenna's café to eat but they wanted to spend time together by the waterfall. She did want to invite Miss Addie to her wedding and made it a point to tell Rusty so. He suggested they discuss the details while eating their food.

Nora laid a blanket out on the bank by the water, listening to the flowing waters cascading into the creek. The sound was surreal, so relaxing after hours on a hard bench seat. The two ate in silence, listening to the moving water, enjoying just being together.

When she finished her meal, Nora began to pack up. Rusty reached over to take her hand. He leaned in, tasting her lips in a gentle, loving way. Nora almost blushed at his tender touch. "When would you like to have the ceremony?"

She sat back. "A week from Sunday?"

Rusty's face dropped. "That far away? Why, what am I gonna do for a whole week and a half?"

"Same thing as always, Rusty. We have a ranch to run."

He shook his head back and forth as if disappointed. "I'm not gonna like to have to sleep out in my old cot, waiting to come to the house for over a week."

Nora sighed. "You never complained before about your sleeping quarters! Why, I made sure you had the best bed in the bunk house. I even sewed that calico print curtain to run across your area so you had your own space!"

Rusty guffawed when Nora got riled. He leaned in and gave her a quick kiss on the cheek. "I like my bunk, Nora. It's just going to be lonely because you won't be there beside me."

Nora blushed. In his own way, Rusty tried to be romantic. Except some of the things he said riled her to no end. Oh, well, no one understood him like she did. She placed both her hands on his face and pulled him in for a long, sweet kiss. "Take that!" she said before turning away to gather up the picnic supplies.

Rusty whipped off his hat and threw it in the air. "Whoo! If you are gonna kiss me like that then I'm going to make sure you get riled up each and every day!"

Nora laughed so hard she almost doubled over, tears streaming down her cheeks.

After packing up, they went to town to pick up some supplies in Wichita Falls. Nora could not for the life of her hide the smile across her face.

She had that same silly smile on her face when Miss Addie let her in and directed her towards the table. A hot cup of tea was placed in front of her. As she added the sweetener, Nora wondered if Miss Addie had ever been in love. She didn't have the heart to ask but it was on her mind. The woman who was responsible for bringing in many mail order brides to the territory had to have been in love at one time or other.

"How was your adventure, Miss Nora?"

"It was indeed an adventure. I've gotten engaged."

Miss Addie's brow rose. "Interesting! May I ask to whom?"

Nora smiled. "You know who. You were right all along."

The older woman nodded in agreement. "Congratulations are in order. When will the wedding be?"

"A week from Sunday. You have my personal invitation."

"Thank you, dear. I will be there. Will the pastor from Cooper's Ridge be officiating the ceremony?"

"I certainly hope so. I plan to find out as soon as we get back to the ranch today. I can let you know."

Miss Addie placed the tea cup on the table. Her fingers steepled. "Very good. I will want to speak with him after the ceremony. I have a proposition for the town of Cooper's Ridge that may be of interest to him."

"There is a lack of women there, if you are planning what I think you are," Nora offered. When she had been there, the ratio of women to men was not good at all.

"I am hoping to help build up Coopers Ridge in the same way Wichita Falls and Mill's Ridge has been developing."

Nora wondered why she wanted to include Coopers Ridge since she didn't have a monetary stake in the new town. Unless, she was planning to purchase some real estate.

She admired Miss Addie. The woman was a fine business woman with smarts. Not many women of her age were a success. She had started this town many years ago, helping to build it up with her investments and mail order brides to bring peace to an unruly area. It had worked.

"I'm sure Cooper is open to building up his town. It has been a pleasure, Miss Addie, but I have a need to be on my way. I've been away way too long."

Her hostess stood, then gave her a hug. "Welcome back, Nora. I'm glad you found all the answers you needed."

She turned one last time before leaving the boarding house. "Oh, I've found more answers than I'll ever need," she mentioned, heartbroken at the thought of the secret Rusty revealed. It didn't upset as much as it did, but she knew when she got home there would be a private visit to Widow Young's ranch.

Five miles from Wichita Falls Rusty ordered her to slow the wagon. Several men in the distance were riding their horses hard. When they saw the wagon, they slowed down. One of the men slowly moved his hand towards his holster.

Rusty rode along side the wagon, reaching in to pull out the shotgun under the bench. He laid it across his lap before riding in front of the now slowly moving wagon. He shielded Nora from the view but she wasn't about to sit back on the bench and do nothing.

Reaching inside her boot, Nora grabbed her small pistol, hiding it inside the pocket of her dress where she'd have a better reach. She had more hiding in the wagon than anyone would ever know.

Nora knew the dangers of traveling away from the ranch and she was always prepared. "I got you covered, Rusty."

"I know you do, Nora. Stay calm, they may mean no harm."

Nora knew an outlaw when she saw one. The three men who rode up to their wagon were bad men. She had interviewed many ranch hands over the years, men who wanted to hide out on her ranch so the law wouldn't find them. She had turned every one of them away, usually while holding a shotgun and warning them to never touch foot on her land again.

That's one thing Nora never tolerated. Trouble. It looked as if these men were passing through, perhaps wanting to rob them blind. She wasn't about to let them.

"Ho there!" Rusty called out. The men stopped in front of Rusty, a few feet back from the wagon. Nora stood in the wagon, pointing the pistol over Rusty's shoulder.

"Be on your way," she told the riders. "There's nothing here you want."

Rusty turned. "No need for that yet," he told her, nodding to the shotgun in his lap, letting her know in no uncertain terms he had things under control.

She didn't stand down for no one. Not any more. Since her husbands secrets all came out, she wasn't about to have any bad men do terrible things in her presence any longer. Nor was she going to be shot in the back by a bandit or worse.

"We are passing by, ma'am," the tall man in the saddle told her. "Your husband is right. No need to point that gun at us."

He reached up to take off his wide-rimmed hat. The man was thin, his sandy hair greased down, a part on the side. A thick moustache rode over his upper lip, pointing upward at the tips.

"One can never be sure," she told him, although she softened somewhat when he called Rusty her husband. He wasn't quite yet, but she liked the way it sounded. Still, she wasn't about to let her guard down.

He tipped his hat. "I can't agree more. We're in a hurry so if you don't mind, can you point that gun in another direction so we may pass by peaceably?"

"Not on your life," she told him, a sweet smile on her face. It didn't reach her eyes and he gave her a long stare before nodding.

Rusty coughed. "Ride on, gentleman."

The moustached man tipped his hat, dug in his heels and waved the others on. "Let's go, men!"

Horse's hooves stirred up the dirt as the three riders headed in the direction of Wichita Falls. Nora kept her hand on the trigger until they were far enough away she was able to relax.

Rusty touched her sleeve. "You did good, Nora. They're gone."

"Do you think we should go back to Wichita Falls and warn them?"

"The sheriff can't do anything unless they committed a crime. They may skirt around the town. It doesn't look like they'll be stopping there, look."

He pointed as the riders took a left away from town. Nora was relieved. She didn't want anyone to get hurt and those men didn't look as if they were there to visit. They were up to no good. The only reason they didn't try to rob or hurt Rusty and herself was because they were well armed. That didn't mean they wouldn't circle around to try to steal their provisions later.

"We should keep an eye out. I'll ride behind again, Nora. You be careful."

Rusty turned around, leaned down to give her a swift kiss and fell behind, taking up the rear again. Just as he did so, a group of riders came over the hill. They stopped once again. Nora stood, prepared to produce her pistol one more time.

"Rusty!"

"I see them, slow down, Nora. It looks like the law."

It was the law. Several men produced badges claiming to be Texas Rangers. "Junius Peak, Texas Ranger here, sir. Ma'am." He tipped his hat, aware of the rifle sitting across Rusty's lap.

Nora relaxed. She sat back down on the bench to let Rusty take care of this. Her interest was in getting back home. They were only about a half hour away.

"Did you happen to see any of these men pass by?" He held out a wanted poster. When Rusty nodded Nora peeked to see the face of the man who had just crossed their path less than five minutes ago.

"Sure did," Rusty told him. "And the one in your other hand was with him, too. They headed east instead of going into the town of Wichita Falls."

"How long ago?"

"Approximately less than five minutes or so."

The Texas Ranger tipped his hat, waving to the others. "Let's ride, boys!"

They watched the group of riders head the same way. "Wonder what that was all about?"

Rusty shrugged. "Outlaws."

Nora sat down, ready to keep moving. "I wasn't able to read the poster. You were closer, Rusty, did you see who they are?"

He nodded. "Sure did. Sam Bass, wanted for robbing a train was all I seen. The other wanted man was Jim Murphy. Didn't catch why he was wanted. I'd say we got lucky back there."

Nora agreed. "Let's go home, Rusty. This has been quite the exhilarating experience."

"Sure has," he told her, replacing the shotgun under the seat. When he leaned in he gave her another kiss.

Nora grinned. "You going to keep kissing me like this when we are married?"

"Even more so. I'm going to woo you like you ain't never been, Nora White. You wait and see."

Chapter 9

Rusty was glad to see the old battered wooden sign ahead. It had been quite the journey even though so many things had happened. In his own way, he was glad they had this opportunity to spend time together away from the ranch, now it felt better to be home.

The wagon turned down the lane towards the White Ranch. There was a slight breeze moving the large wooden sign back and forth. Rusty made a note of getting the sign re-painted.

This time of day everyone would be out working on the ranch. Rusty looked out over the land and took in a deep breath.

"We're home," he said, his voice so low he didn't think Nora heard over the clip-clop of the horses.

She pulled back on the reins, stopping the wagon, gazing over the hundreds of acres of ranch land they called home. "Yes, we are. Isn't it beautiful? I'm glad we got away, Rusty, but here is where my heart belongs. Here on this land, with you. I swear it's always been the two of us. I didn't allow myself to believe we belonged together."

It was a moment in time he'd never forget. The slight wind stirred up, rustling a few nearby branches from the trees lining the path that would lead them home. She reached out a hand as he worked his way to her side. Looking down at her sitting so proud, he leaned in the wagon and kissed her cheek.

No words were spoken after that kiss. They looked out over the land, holding hands for the longest time.

Three riders came over the horizon riding hell-bent for leather towards the front yard. Something was wrong! Nora straightened, moving the wagon forward, pushing the horses as fast as she could. "Go ahead of me, Rusty! Find out what's happened."

He took off down the road without hesitation, cutting across the yard, racing towards the three men on horseback. The riders stopped at Luke's cabin, jumping from their mounts. The sun was in his eyes even though the wide brimmed hat shaded the rays, his vision was blurred. It did look as if Nora's sons were standing on the front porch of Luke's cabin pacing back and forth.

The baby! Luke's wife was in labor! He gazed back to see Nora running across the yard, her wagon already being taken care of by one of the ranch hands.

"What a welcome, Nora! I think the baby is about to make its way into the world." He got down from his horse, waiting for her to catch up. She brushed right by him but not before turning and giving him one of those lovely smiles of hers.

It was back to business for Nora. She took charge of the situation, hugging each of her sons, reassuring Luke everything would be alright and let herself into the cabin to help with the delivery.

Rusty made his way to the boys. "Luke, you'll wear a hole in the floorboards pacing back and forth."

A clump of hair fell over Luke's brow. He tried to push it away from his face. "I knew she was feeling bad this morning and I left anyway. We had to check on some cattle so we rode out earlier than usual. Callie said she tripped and fell in the yard on the way to the kitchen. I think it brought on the labor pains." Luke's face was filled with remorse.

Rusty had to do something. "Come on, now, boy! It's not your fault, snap out of it! She's going to have the baby whether you are here to keep an eye on her or not."

Samuel and Adam agreed even though neither one knew anything about having a child.

Luke sighed. "I guess you're right. Welcome home, Rusty! I'm glad you're back. And Ma, too!"

He went back to pacing back and forth again as if his life depended on it. Rusty had to smile. "Looks like we made it back just in time! Ain't nothing I can do about your nerves, so I'm going to put away my horse and come sit with you."

"I'll take care of your horse, Rusty." Samuel patted him on the back. "Why don't you have a seat and rest. I'm sure it's been a long ride."

Rusty gave Samuel a nod. It had been a long morning. With the chance of those outlaws circling back and the long ride home, he didn't realize how tired he was. He wasn't getting any younger. Ten years ago a journey like he'd been on was nothing to him. He guessed times had changed.

An hour later, Luke knocked on the door of the cabin. The women locked him out earlier when he heard his wife scream and he tried to bust in. Rusty grinned when he heard a chorus of women tell Luke to calm down and wait.

He sat on the rocker on the porch watching Nora's son wait for the birth of his first born child. Luke was always the serious one, probably because he had to be. Rusty remembered how Robert would put a lot more on the oldest than the other two. It was no wonder he had the type of personality he did. Luke tended to be over dramatic at times but Rusty didn't care. He was a fine man and Rusty was glad he got to watch him grow over the years. Was this how a father felt about a son?

Rusty had a brief marriage many years ago and produced a daughter, who now lived a wonderful life with her husband in Montana. She wrote now and again but was settled and didn't travel much to see him any more. He had always wanted sons but his wife had died in child birth. He had raised his daughter up to be a fine woman and when she married, he was never more proud of her.

The years he spent on this ranch helping Nora's boys grow and teaching them the things they'd need made him feel as if he did have sons of his own.

That's why when Nora flung open the door and announced there was a healthy baby boy he held his breath until she reassured everyone Abigail was fine, too.

Rusty slowly made his way to Nora's side. She watched him for a moment. "You look a little pale, Rusty. Are you thinking about your first wife?"

"For a moment or two." He placed a hand on her cheek. "I'm glad everything is alright. I'm going to check on the barn."

Adam was rocking back and forth. "The barn's fine, Rusty. What's gotten into you?"

"Hush, Adam," Nora told her middle son.

He ignored Adam's words and headed toward the barn. A little time with his animals would make him feel better. Rusty hadn't realized all these emotions would arise again after so many years squashing them inside.

Before he went in the barn, he gazed back to see Nora watching him from the porch, concern on her face. He lifted a hand to wave to let her know he was okay. She nodded but still continued to stare.

He needed a few moments alone. Rehashing the past was a terrible thing that needed to be dealt with and move on from. It was better to do alone.

Except Nora would not allow him to squander his day feeling sorry for himself. An hour later, he felt her presence while he was in one of the stalls brushing down a mare. The brushing motion was calming, it always settled his nerves.

A small coo came from the little bundle Nora held in her arms. "I thought you would come back to see the little fellow but you didn't."

"Got busy in here, Nora." He placed the brush on a shelf and left the stall, being drawn to the little baby bundled in her arms. He placed his hands on his knees as he bent over to get close to Luke's son.

"He's a fine looking specimen."

"Specimen?" Nora shook her head. "Oh, Rusty, he's a baby!"

Rusty looked up at her and grinned. "May I?"

"Of course. Why don't you have a seat on the hay bale there first."

"Oh, Nora, stop being so bossy. I know how to hold a tiny little one." He placed his hands on the bundle and picked up the baby as if he had tons of experience doing so. His brow rose when he gazed at his bride to be. "See?"

She touched his arm. "I do see. You make a fine grandfather."

Rusty held back a tear or two. He felt as if this little feller was his grand son. The love that tugged at his heart watching his tiny face sleep was overwhelming. Rusty wasn't able to speak for several minutes.

Nora sighed. "The moment I held him, I had the same reaction. Can you believe we've come this far, Rusty? It's always been you and I, hasn't it? Robert was dead in my heart and soul a long, long time ago. I just didn't want to let go of our dream to build this ranch up. But, you were the one there for me. He is truly your grand son."

"Ah, Nora. Thank you for those words. It means the world to me to hear you say this."

"I mean every single word. I haven't spoken to the boys yet about our marriage ceremony. I didn't want to overshadow their joy today. We'll tell them tomorrow."

Rusty shook his head. "I think we should tell them now, Nora. Because they'll want to hear it from us and not find out when I am dancing you around the yard in the moonlight tonight!"

Nora giggled like a school girl. She held out her arms for the baby. "I think we better take the child back to its mother. He is probably getting hungry."

Rusty looked down at the little feller before handing him back. "What did they name him?"

Nora headed out the barn. "I'll let Luke and Abigail tell you. Come on, Rusty, let's take this baby back and tell our family the good news!"

<> <>

Nora placed the little one beside his mother. Abigail was exhausted but Luke helped her position the baby so he was able to feed.

Rusty stood inside the cabin alongside Nora. They waited for some time before Adam, Melody, Samuel and Callie showed up.

When everyone was present, Abigail spoke up. "We wanted to tell you all at once what we decided to name our child and perhaps explain things so no one gets upset at our decision."

Nora glanced at Rusty before speaking. "The child is yours alone to name, darling. We just want to hear what you've decided."

Luke stood, his face so serious it worried Rusty. "I always thought when I'd have a child I would name him or her after one of my parents. Abigail and I have been talking for the last hour and I realized that not all parents are natural."

Rusty frowned. "What the heck are you talking about?"

Nora nudged him with her elbow.

"Rusty, since I've been a kid, you've been like a father to me. I'm not going to tell you how my own father was because we all know he wasn't worthy of his name. You replaced my own father when he died. Even before. My brothers and I feel as if you have taken the place of the man called Robert White and have done a better job than he ever could or would have if he hadn't died. Therefore, I'd like to introduce you to my son, Russell White, named after his grandfather Rusty."

This time a tear fell. Rusty never cried in front of anyone, this time he just didn't care. "I am honored," he said, his voice raspy, emotional.

Nora placed a hand on his arm. "I suppose it is time to tell you some more good news. We didn't want to mention it today because of the child's birth but Rusty felt as if you would want to know right away. I believe he is right."

"Ma, I think we already know but we want to hear it from the two of you." Luke was smiling. When Rusty glanced at Adam and Samuel they had that same grin on their faces. The women stood by their husband's side watching the scene play out.

Rusty raised his hands in the air. "We're getting hitched! Your Ma and I, a week from Sunday!"

Nora laughed at the way he made his announcement.

The baby gurgled a little bit so Rusty assumed he was just as happy as the rest of them.

Each man shook Rusty's hand. "Congratulations, Rusty. We hoped someday but now that someday is here, Ma chose the best man for the job." Luke gave his Ma a hug next.

Nora pushed Luke back and placed a hand on her hip. "You saying it's going to be a job for Rusty to be married to me?"

Luke flung his head back and laughed. "Oh, Ma! You know what I meant!" He gave her another hug and whispered in her ear. "You know you are my favorite Ma."

"Do you hear this, Rusty? My own son using my own words back at me."

Rusty had to speak up. "Well, Nora, I heard you say those same words to him many times. Come to think of it, I heard you say it to Adam and Samuel."

They all laughed, careful not to be too loud as the little bundle of joy was fast asleep in Abigail's arms.

Nora called out to the girls. "We best get supper started. I'm sure everyone is famished by now."

As Nora, Melody and Callie walked through the yard to the main house, Rusty stood outside on the porch feeling like one of the luckiest men alive.

Another tear fell as he looked over to the horizon. No words would ever explain the feeling of total surrender he felt when thinking of his grandson, Russell.

Rusty always thought of the ranch as home. Now, he knew that even though the boy wasn't blood, the legacy of the White Ranch would go on even after he was gone.

What more could a father ask for?

What more could a grandfather ask?

It was a darn good feeling.

Chapter 10

Nora didn't want to wait until morning to have a talk with the widow but by the time supper was finished she was entirely too exhausted to ride over to the small farm.

Luke had taken supper to his wife, anxious to get back to his family. Nora gazed at the cabin where one small light glowed through the window like a beacon in the night, so proud of her first born son. She rocked back and forth on her favorite chair on the front porch. "I'm happy now. It's been over a week and a half since I was able to sit here and look at all God's glory."

Rusty sat beside her on his favorite wooden chair. He nodded at first, then began to rock back and forth for some time before the rocker stilled. His eyes were closed, his breathing even. Nora thought it odd that he wasn't snoring since he always did in church.

The sound of the screen door caused him to jerk awake. He grumbled under his breath and stretched his arms over his head.

"Ma, Rusty. We're going to head home." Adam and Melody walked hand in hand across the yard towards their own cabin. Next, Callie came outside to fetch her husband. They were working on a cabin but it wasn't quite finished yet. Samuel had been sitting on the steps waiting on her to finish the dishes before going upstairs to bed.

"Goodnight."

"Goodnight Samuel. Callie."

Rusty yawned. "I must've fell asleep. Nora, how long are you going to sit outside staring into the sky?"

She shook her head. "I may sit here all night. It's gorgeous, isn't it? I didn't realize how much I missed this part of the day."

"Yes, it certainly is but a man's got to have his sleep. Goodnight, Nora." He leaned over for a sweet kiss. "I love you."

"I love you, Rusty."

She watched as he turned the corner, heading towards the bunk house. Then he turned around and walked back to her, his strides long and full of purpose. His boots clunked on the stairs as he made his way to her side. "I almost forgot."

Nora giggled as Rusty took her hand, guiding her out on the lawn. The moon peeked out from the dark night, stars sprinkled so far and wide the sky looked never-ending. He placed a hand on her waist and took her other hand in his, holding it close to his chest.

He began to hum first then shuffled his feet, guiding her around in circles and swaying back and forth. Their dance lasted for a long time as it became slower and their bodies melded closer. Before long, they were barely moving their feet, their arms wrapped tight around each other.

"We should go in now," Nora told him, enjoying being in his arms.

"We should've got married in Dallas, Nora. I told you so," he mumbled.

"Does it matter if we are married or not, Rusty? I love you and as far as I'm concerned you've been like a husband to me and a father to the boys. They even recognize it as such."

He pressed his cheek to hers. "Temptation is trying its hardest to follow you inside, but I'm a man of honor. I already made up my mind you will be romanced and courted like a true queen. And do you know why?"

She shook her head. "Why, Rusty?"

"Because you are a woman who deserves to be treated this way. I won't damage your honor by sleeping with you before the wedding no matter how old we are."

Nora smiled. "Don't you think it's a little bit silly, considering we are adults well into our middle age?"

"Nope! Let me ask you this, Nora. Did Robert court you? Did he dance with you under the moonlight?"

She looked at him. "Oh, Rusty. You know darn well Robert wasn't a romantic man. At least not with me. Our marriage was more or less arranged by our parents. He lived on the farm beside ours. We always knew our parents wanted us married so that's what we did. Then we started this ranch and never had time for anything else. I never thought about romance with him."

Rusty nodded. "Well, see now, life as you know it is about to change. I am wooing you, Nora, and there won't be any arguing with me. I plan to show you romance from now on until we are both dead and buried. We'll sleep together on our wedding night and not one moment before."

Nora was touched, even if his wording was silly. No one wants to be reminded someday they would be dead and buried. Still, she had to give him a chance. "Okay, Rusty. I'll allow you to romance me. Now if we aren't going to go any further than a dance, I'll bid you good night."

She placed a quick kiss on his cheek and hurried to the front door, waving goodnight as she closed the screen door.

Nora sat on the hillside, staring at the parcel of land belonging to the Youngs. Acres of farmland and rolling hills covered the area further than the eye could see. Nora was reminded of how Robert would ride here every single afternoon to help a poor widow. Or, so she thought.

Even though bitterness tried to fill her up, she wasn't going to allow it any longer. If anyone should feel dishonored, it was Widow Young.

Shame fluttered through her blood, knowing it was her husband who had hurt this woman. How awful for a young woman to be treated in such a way. It was almost too much for Nora. She went to turn her horse around, to leave and let things lie but the widow must've seen her silhouette from the window and stood outside on the porch, a shotgun resting in her arms.

It was barely daylight. Nora had saddled her mare before breakfast, while the moon was starting to descend into the abyss and before the sun tried to peek its way through the clouds. She started down the hill, determined to say her peace.

It was time.

The widow deserved some peace of her own.

"Nora White, what do you want."

Nora didn't blame her for being blunt and to the point. The last time she had spoken to the widow, Nora had told her to never step foot on her land.

"I know what happened."

Widow Young shifted her stance. She wasn't quite as stiff as a moment ago. "We had this discussion at your ranch. I don't ever intend to step foot there again and I ask the same of you. Get off my land."

"One of your ranch hands told one of ours what really happened. That you weren't at fault. He saw it happen several times. My dead husband forced you against your will."

The moment her words were out the widow broke down as if something inside of her burst apart. Tears streamed down her face. She set the rifle across the wooden chair on the porch and covered her face. "Go on, get out of here!"

Nora slipped from her mare and went to the widow, putting her arms around the smaller lady. "I'm so sorry. I didn't know. No one knew."

"I hated him! I see his face every day because my boys look like him. I want to scream some nights because I had no choice. Back then, I was vulnerable, he took what he wanted and laughed when I said I would tell you."

"If I'd have known, he'd been dead much earlier than when the cattle rustlers got to him."

"That's not what he told me, Nora. He said you knew and didn't care because you no longer let him in your bed."

Nora shook with fury. "That was a lie. He was an awful, horrible man. I had no idea just how much. I'm ashamed, Widow Young, so ashamed for what he did to you."

They spoke for a long time. Widow Young made some coffee and they sat at her kitchen table discussing everything that had happened over the years.

It was like a cleanse in a brook of cooling spring water. Nora reached in her skirt pocket and pulled out a folded letter. Another secret, another lie.

"Is that what I think it is?" the widow asked.

"It is. This is the original loan Robert gave you so long ago when your husband died. A loan I knew nothing about. When he died I put two of his personal boxes in a drawer. I didn't have the energy or time to go through them, not thinking there was anything of importance in them so I had never looked. If I had, I would've known he loaned you the money to save your farm soon after your husband passed away."

"I'm sorry. I thought you knew."

Nora shook her head. "I did not. He had a notebook of the money you borrowed and your payments to him. Then the payments stopped. I wasn't able to understand why until I saw this document."

Widow Young's face went white. She stuttered for a moment before hiding her face in her hands. "Oh, God! He lied to me, told me he ripped it up. I have the original deed. He made me think this was my land all along but it wasn't. I've been working this land all these years and it belongs to you!" Widow Young flung her head down, covering her face with her arms sobbing like Nora had never heard a woman cry before.

"Where are your boys?" Nora asked, thinking she may need their help to calm the widow down. This was all new to her, trying to be nice to a woman she had hated for years.

"They've gone to Wichita Falls. I'm here alone. Alone. Like always." She began to sob again.

Nora didn't know what to do. "Now, stop, Widow Young! You stop right this minute!" She took the widow by the arm and made her stand up. "Follow me!"

When Nora got her outside, she forced the widow to take some deep breaths. When she had calmed, Nora pointed to the chair. "Sit."

"I guess you can tell me what to do since I don't own a darn thing any more." She sat, her shoulders slumped, defeat in her eyes.

Nora sat in the other chair, pulling the widow's hands into hers. "Now you listen to me. You are a strong woman. How else would you have survived all these years. But you are tired and don't deserve to suffer so."

"I have nothing left. How do I tell my boys?"

"You don't have to."

"What?" Her tear streaked face stared at Nora hard.

"I don't want your land. My husband tricked you. As I studied his notes last night, I learned you had been making payments long before he started to demand favors from you. When you failed to make the last few payments, he made you sign over the land to him. But you didn't sign off on the real deed. You still have it, right?"

Widow Young nodded. "I do. He had a new one made up. I signed it with his promise no one would ever know as long as I -"

"Hush, don't say it. He said that because he wanted you to believe the land was no longer yours. He wrote up a new one but never had time to get it done properly. Maybe he would have done it but he died before the new deed he showed you was properly executed. Here." Nora handed her the fake deed.

A new hope surged in the widow's eyes. "Truly?"

Nora grinned. "Yes, let's burn this one."

It didn't take long for the widow to light the document and set it aflame. The two stared at the embers, each having their own thoughts on the matter.

Nora spoke first. "I'm sorry what he did to you, how he lied. He was a disturbed man. I had no idea. We were so busy building the ranch, it had been a shock when he had admitted to have cheated on me. He swore it happened only once and pretended to be so guilt ridden I forgave him. Then I forbid him to ever step foot on your farm again but he did anyway behind my back. We were both fools."

"Thank you, Nora. We've wasted so many years being angry at each other."

"Well, no longer. Our feud has come to an end. Agreed?"

The widow nodded, wiping her tear streaked face on her sleeve. "Yes, agree."

"I do wonder about one thing though. Widow Young, why did you accept money from my boys knowing all this? You allowed them to pay you off to keep silent about who the twins father truly was?"

She looked guilty. "I'm sorry. After Robert died, they found out the twins were from their own father. They came to me and offered me money to keep it quiet. They never wanted you to know what he had done. When the boys got older, I told them the truth but I never told anyone else. I took the money because of the deed. I feared someday you would uncover the truth and throw me off this land with nothing to my name. I stashed it away in case. Stay here, I'll be right back."

Nora understood now, more so than ever. She probably would've done the same thing, maybe even worse.

The widow returned with a bag and handed it to Nora. "I don't need this any longer. I have my land, it's all I need."

Nora peered in the bag. Piles of money from all the years her own boys paid the widow to keep the secret were stuffed in the bag. She was amazed.

"I have an idea."

"No. The money is yours. I never intended to keep it unless you threw me off the land. Honestly, I was hoping you'd never find out about the deed. You were so busy running your ranch, I prayed every single night you'd never know."

Nora gave her another hug. "That had to be horrible for you. To have to place your head on your pillow at night, not knowing if you'll have a home the next morning. My boys all are married now, they found good women and built their own cabins on the ranch. We are all one big happy family."

The widow stared at her as if Nora's words meant nothing. "I don't know what to say."

"You don't have to say anything." She pushed the bag of money her way. "Take this money and have two cabins built. Your boys deserve happy lives. Let's get the matchmaker Miss Addie to find each one of them a wife of their own. Widow Young, you want to see them married and happy with little children running around on this land, don't you?"

The widow smiled, her eyes lighting up at the thought of grandchildren. "That would be a dream come true."

Nora patted her hand. "We can make it happen. Come to my wedding next Sunday at noon. I'll introduce you to Miss Addie."

The widow stood. "Your wedding? Nora? You?"

"I met a man that I realized I've been in love with all my life."

A smile splayed across the widow's cheeks. "Who is it?"

"Rusty the wrangler and ranch hand that I've known since we started this ranch. He has been by my side more so than Robert ever was. I've enjoyed a grand adventure with him and now he is going to woo me until we are married next Sunday."

The widow gave her a hug. "Thank you for this talk. Now, go on, get back to your ranch and let that man woo you."

Nora got on her mare, satisfied their talk ended so well. "I was worried you'd shoot me right off my horse. I'm glad you didn't."

"You're a brave woman, Nora White. I'm glad I didn't either."

Nora turned away and waved as she made her way towards her own land. A lone figure came towards her and she knew right away who it was.

Rusty stopped when she waved. He took his hat off, slapped it against his thigh and wiped the sweat from his brow. The man had known she was going to come here. It was like he read her mind, knew her actions and the way she thought.

He amazed her. Every single day. How had she not seen it years ago?

"Howdy," he said when she caught up to him.

"Hi," she told him, a wicked look in her eye.

Rusty sat back in the saddle. "You've got that look in your eye, Nora White."

"What look? The one that says I'm going to win this race?" She started out before he got a chance to follow, racing her mare, heading towards the creek where they often stopped to watch the water gently flow down the stream. She knew her boys had come here too. It was a special place of peace and serenity.

"Yahoo!" Rusty yelled, riding alongside her, looking over with a big grin. "You best giddy on up if you think you can win," he teased and took off full force.

Nora knew he had the better horse but she tried to keep up anyway. In a moment, he'd slow down and pretend she was going to pass. He always let her win. Always. There wasn't a time he hadn't. She knew the routine.

She watched the big stallion slow down a little. It was hardly noticeable but Nora knew. She came up alongside him, nodding and then took off to beat him to the creek.

They sat side by side, holding hands while the water lapped against the rocks and stones, filtering through and making its way downstream.

Rusty squeezed her hand. "Did you get things straight with the widow?"

"She's actually a nice person. We've wasted too many years feuding and becoming bitter enemies. I've said my peace and the end result is she is coming to our wedding next Sunday in hopes to speak with Miss Addie about the twins."

"Interesting. How do you think the boys will react?"

Nora shrugged. "They'll be happy we made things right. I'm not sure I should give them all the details but it's time to have a talk with them. They need to get to know their brothers."

"I'm in agreement with you. I think the twins want the same thing."

Nora stared at Rusty's profile. "How do you know this, Rusty? You wouldn't unless you've been speaking to them."

"I don't want you to get excited now, Nora. A few times the twins came to me asking how to do something. I never turned them away."

Instead of getting upset, she gave him a kiss. "You are a man of honor. Those boys had no man to look up to but you tried, didn't you, Rusty? You never even had to."

He sighed. "This is my home. Like you, it's where my heart lies. No matter what Robert had done, I felt it my place to try to pick up the pieces of his disaster. We all tried to keep you from knowing how horrible a man he was. Maybe we shouldn't have but it did lead to a grand adventure, didn't it?"

He kissed her gently, his weathered face covering her sweet lips. Birds chirped on cue. The sun began to beat down, warming the morning air. She smiled against his lips. It had indeed been a grand adventure.

<> <>

Nora wore her wedding gown, a cream-colored dress of simple cotton material. The sleeves flared open at the wrist and along the matching covering.

She wore her hair down. Even the younger women sighed when they saw her standing at the screen door ready to make her way to the alter.

Callie gave her a hug. "With your hair down, you look ten years younger, Nora. Here." Callie handed her four long stemmed roses, two in pink and two in white. The thorns were carefully removed so she wasn't pricked by them.

Melody straightened out the train in the back. She hugged Nora the longest. "I'm glad you are finally going to be happy."

Abigail gave her a hug with one hand while Russell slept in her other arm. "I love you, Nora."

She turned to stare at the three women who were now her daughters. "I love all three of you and that little baby boy. There is going to be lots of changes in the years ahead, ladies, so hang on tight because there are two more Young-White men to marry off."

They all giggled at the inside joke. Nora had told them how her and the widow were planning to make sure the Young men found a mail order bride also.

The three ladies walked towards the guests first, sitting in the front row while Nora made her way alone down the aisle towards Rusty, who stood at the alter alongside Pastor Murphy.

Nora almost burst out laughing when Rusty threw a glance at Cooper, glaring at him and then puffing his chest as if to say he got the goods after all. She shook her head, unable to hide the smile displayed on her face.

Rusty took her hand, staring at the roses for a moment before pulling one from the small bunch. He tore off some of the long stem and gently placed it in her hair. "Perfect," he told her before turning back to the Pastor for the official ceremony.

"You may kiss the bride," Cooper finally told him and boy did he. Rusty made a big show of leaning Nora back and laying a kiss on her that she was wide-eyed when he stood her upright.

She placed a hand over her mouth. "Oh, my, Rusty," then realized he was showing off for the pastor's sake.

Pastor Cooper wasn't even paying attention. Nora turned her head slightly to see what he was looking at. Interestingly, he had his eyes on the Widow Young. She was in the second row, sitting between her twin boys, trying to hide between them. The widow was shy but when she spotted the pastor staring, a blush the size of two ripe apples covered her cheeks.

Nora turned back to Rusty. "You can stop showing off to the pastor," she whispered in his ear. "He has his eye on someone else."

"I'll never stop showing the world how much I love you," Rusty told her, bending her back for another deep kiss. The crowd began to clap.

Nora straightened up, laughing, then turned and threw her small bouquet of flowers into the crowd.

It was said whoever caught them would be the next to marry. She had purposely pointed them in the direction of the widow but instead, one of the twins caught them. He looked shocked and passed them off to the other twin brother, who then laid them in the widow's lap. They all three laughed.

"Everything is going to be alright," Nora told Rusty, giving him a swift kiss of her own.

As they turned from the alter she began to laugh. Out in the yard were her three boys, piled on top of each other, wrestling as if they were thirteen again, their wives turning to stare at the ruckus.

Nora swept past the ladies, reaching out to touch the baby's cheek, knowing the legacy of the White family would continue on.

She called back to her husband who hurried along to catch up with her. "I love you, Rusty."

"I love you, my dear Nora. Always have, always will."

Thank you for reading Nora's story. At first, I was planning on matching her with Cooper Murphy from Coopers Ridge until my readers wanted to see Rusty and Nora together. It just happened anyway and I'm glad the two got to spend the rest of their lives together.

What's next for this series? Well, the widow and Miss Addie are probably holding a long conversation at the moment, trying to decide if the twins are ready to marry, starting with Russell.

Now Available A Bride for Russell[1]

(https://www.amazon.com/Bride-Russell-Sons-Nora-White-ebook/

dp/B07DYFLQYJ/

ref=as_li_ss_tl?ie=UTF8&linkCode=ll1&tag=keysvaca-

20&linkId=317570a3845518a2b34a7b3b2917c813)

---

1. https://www.amazon.com/Bride-Russell-Sons-Nora-White-

ebook/dp/B07DYFLQYJ/

ref=as_li_ss_tl?ie=UTF8&linkCode=ll1&tag=keysvaca-

20&linkId=317570a3845518a2b34a7b3b2917c813

Sign up for my emails to find out when each story comes out. Go to www.cyndiraye.com[2]

---

2. http://www.cyndiraye.com

Don't miss out!

Visit the website below and you can sign up to receive emails whenever Cyndi Raye publishes a new book. There's no charge and no obligation.

https://books2read.com/r/B-A-PXQ-WCWFC

BOOKS 2 READ

Connecting independent readers to independent writers.

www.ingramcontent.com/pod-product-compliance
Lightning Source LLC
Chambersburg PA
CBHW022159150726
47992CB00002B/873